Crossed Out

Malcolm Hollingdrake

Book Six in the Harrogate Crime Series

Praise for Malcolm Hollingdrake

The quality of writing was excellent and I'm looking forward to reading the next in the series – which is already on my Kindle.

Mark Tilbury - Author

All in all, gripping and engrossing with a cast of characters I look forward to reading about again.

Eva Mercx – Novel Delights

This book has a tremendous story, that I can't stop thinking about 2 days after I finished it.

Susan Hampson – Books From Dusk Till Dawn

The author knows how to write one intriguing plot that is very well researched, that will have the reader hooked from start to finish.

Shell Baker – Chelle's Book Reviews

This book is professionally written and totally gripping. I read it within twenty-four hours because I couldn't put it down.

Jill Burkinshaw – Books n All

The story is very well told and the writing excellent. All of these points add up to making Game Point a book you can easily read in one sitting.

Neats Wilson – Life Of A Nerdish Mum

Again, this is another fantastic book in the DCI Bennett series from Malcolm Hollingdrake and I stand by my thoughts that the series gets better as it has progressed – this, hands down the best book in the series.

Donna Maguire – Donnas Book Blog

There is no way to describe Malcolm's new book Dying Art except downright awesome, I was intrigued and compelled by the plotline to savour every moment of what was happening, in the art world and also Bennett's life.

Diane Hogg – Sweet Little Book Blog

I love the characters, the way the story built up. It's so good to see Cyril back again. Malcolm Hollingdrake is one of my favourite authors.

Livia Sbarbaro – Goodreads Reviewer

Dedicated to

Carrie and Brian Heap

Thank you for your friendship.

In memory of

Emily Shutt – an angel, a warrior and a little princess.

God Bless you

xxx

'If anyone would come after me, he must deny himself and take up his cross daily and follow me.'

Luke 9:23

Prologue

The first of April and only a fool would be out at this time in the morning. The fine mist that was often sarcastically referred to as 'dry rain' flushed Harrogate's dark streets and gardens, an organza veil soaking all in its path. Only when trapped momentarily within the streetlights did the drifting, watery sheets appear to be guided invisibly by the slight accompanying breeze. To the lone figure the rain was a bonus; it made the ground forgiving as the fine blade disembowelled a small area of The Stray. A patch of turf and accompanying crocus bulbs, just showing signs of life, formed a small mud mound. Into the cavity was placed a plastic packet and the soil was folded back. Considerately, those bulbs removed were carefully returned. This procedure was no wanton act of vandalism; it was methodical and planned. Once the small cross was connected to the line that linked the buried packet, it was sunk into the ground. His soiled fingers came up to his lips before returning to the top of the cross. The first offering was in place. He stood and bowed. Water droplets ran from his shaved head and down his neck before collecting in cold runnels trapped beneath his clothing. He smiled and walked across the soaked grass, his slight limp barely noticeable.

Chapter One

The blue flashing strobe lights stabbed the morning darkness like fine needles as the ambulance raced along the far side of The Stray. At four a.m., there was no need for the siren. A solitary figure turned to watch it disappear into the distance, a modern-day son et lumière.

A slight, spring-night frost had settled on the grass verge giving an ethereal sheen under the streetlights' sharp, white glow, multi-shadowing the hooded figure as he walked casually along the road, gloved hands stuffed into the marsupial-style pouch at the front of his jacket. He ignored the majority of the domestic waste bins that lined the roadside, left out the previous evening in preparation for the early morning collection. Although all appeared to be the same grey, wheeled clones, they were not. On closer inspection there were differences, many subtle and hardly noticeable in the half-light; some appeared cleaner than others, almost cherished, while others showed signs of complete neglect. The majority had some distinguishing feature that set them apart, made them identifiable, made them belong; a neatly applied house number, some occasional floral stickers, even a set of wickets painted accurately to the lower front. It was the bin daubed gracelessly in red letters by an amateur hand, *Gail's Hair and Nail's,* that he sought. It appeared to have been painted using a hen's foot and contained one too many apostrophes.

He paused and checked the road. All was quiet. A gloved hand lifted the lid whilst the other hand rummaged briefly until a white bin bag was located near the top. Quickly removing it, he stuffed it into his jacket. The lid was closed quietly. Within thirty minutes, the contents would be extracted from the bag and carefully displayed.

***

The crocuses formed their own coloured carpet on either side of the tarmac pathway that linked the corner of Beech Grove and Otley Road to West Park. It was a direct route across The Stray. It was this springtime splendour that brought the many photographers and admirers to Harrogate and today was no exception, aided in part by the clear azure sky and the growing warmth of the sun.

A thin, ethereal mist was released as the early sun melted the morning's frosty coating. Subliming, it rose before quickly vanishing. Angie Rhodes sat alone on the bench, her head back, staring at the sky. She wore an old jacket on which conical studs ran across the right shoulder and down the front, like a protecting row, a barrier of sharp, metal spikes. The left sleeve was untouched apart from a small finger puppet of a white bear stitched to the inner part. However, the right side of the jacket was in total contrast. Numerous, multi-coloured patches had been haphazardly stitched, running down the front and sleeve, making it difficult to see where the sleeve and jacket separated. Skulls, the logo for *A Clockwork Orange,* set on a bright, orange background stood like a threatening beacon next to three braided, coloured bracelets that had been stitched to run in rings round the sleeve, suggestive of an official rank.

Using a small blade, she had for the last fifteen minutes, been amusing herself digging and slicing into her own flesh and she was pleased with the result. Beads of blood from the damaged skin on the back of her hand swelled into small, crimson, jewel-like domes. She raised her hand and admired them before blowing them into red rivulets that quickly crossed the other older scars, spreading like external, vivid veins. She deliberately brought her hand onto her lips and sucked; the metallic flavour was so familiar. She grinned red. It was then that her eyes were drawn to the myriad coloured blooms, a sumptuous border, two feet wide, stretching both to her left and

2

right. She looked for one flower to match the redness of her hand. There was none.

She leaned back on the bench again and stared at the sky. The sun sulled low as if reluctant to rise. The slight breeze, still cool, held its own honed edge against her exposed skin. She lifted the hood of her jacket but remained seated. Her eyes moved slowly, panning the dazzling display in an endeavour to count those blooms directly opposite and stave off the boredom that was growing within, a task encumbered by the occasional breeze that invited some flowers to play hide and seek. She gave up on the task too soon, a trait for which she had always been criticised throughout her school life. Even when she had found employment, she would often lose her concentration and slip away into her own space and time. People did not seem to understand; they did not hear the voices, her voices that could be both friend and foe. They were there at the beginning, encouraging and goading her on but they never seemed to stay when the trouble started. She inserted her finger into the opening of the finger puppet and lifted her arm.

"You can't count them can you, you lazy cow?" She changed her voice and moved her arm pretending that it was the bear which spoke.

"Can't be arsed," she muttered to the bear before sitting back again and stretching her legs across the tarmac path.

"You never could and you never will. Like me, I'm stuck, sewn here in what's usually an upside down fucking world. You didn't think of that when you put needle and thread to work did you? That's 'cos you're thick as pig shit."

She removed her finger and daubed blood on the dirty white of the puppet. "That'll shut you up." She lifted her arm fractionally to see the scarlet contrast with the white. "Bloody bear!"

She closed her eyes briefly, allowing the light to play and dance within the darkness trapped behind her eyelids. She smiled to herself, delighted by the effect and the immediate distraction. Her pleasure, however, was short-lived.

3

"Excuse me. I don't want to squash the flowers."

The voice of Alex Golding was an interruption, an inconvenience that disturbed her puerile amusement. Alex was standing to her right, holding on to the handle of a large pram, waiting for her to move her sprawling legs blocking the pathway. Angie opened her eyes one at a time and simply glared at the young mother. Her face held in the shadow beneath the hood was only partially visible. She reluctantly retracted her legs and as Alex started to move forward she thrust them out again and laughed.

"For a kiss, faggot." She salaciously thrust her tongue in and out of her mouth and leaned forward.

***

Alex felt her heart begin to beat more quickly as the confrontation escalated. She looked directly at the stranger's face cocooned and partially concealed within the hood; a single, blue, tattooed tear was visible below the left eye. A variety of metal rings and studs protruded from her lips and nose.

Alex stared bravely and defiantly at the seated girl before summoning enough strength to confront her. "No? You'll not let me pass, then I'll scream louder than you've heard anyone scream before."

To her relief, Alex saw an immediate change in the young person's attitude, the tongue flicking stopped and the legs were quickly retracted before she pulled the hood over her face, an act of defiance reminiscent of a chastised child. Suddenly she was a bully no longer, she had closed the fabric gate, isolating herself from the outside world. The troublesome woman had been banished to the other side of the fleeced fabric.

Relieved at the youth's submission, Alex moved away quickly along the path.

***

4

Rhodes sat, hooded and hidden, the voices suddenly silenced, she was momentarily invisible to the world. As the sound of footfall receded, she casually stood and turned. The frustration and anger had grown inside her as the voice in her head returned, challenging and goading her.

"Fuck the flowers!" she yelled as loudly as she could.

Alex heard the scream, stopped and turned anxiously. She watched as the youth swung her right leg defiantly in an arc, her foot decapitating a number of the crocuses to the right of the path sending them scattering like confetti across the grass.

"And fuck you, bitch! Fuck you all! Nobody knows, nobody!" She pointed at Alex and showed firstly her fist and then a single finger. "Fuck… everything!"

Quickening her step, Alex Golding, anxious about the youth's next move, turned and walked away from the frustrated anger and wilful destruction. Once she was a safe distance, she waited for her anxiety to calm before telephoning 101 to report the incident to the police.

***

The early sun beamed through the small, wired-glass window that had not been cleaned for an age. Particles of dust floated as if trapped within the light. The contents of the bag taken from the bin were separated carefully; only the longest strands of human hair were then removed from the table where they had originally been spread. The many colours and textures were now mixed; importantly their length was similar. He leaned over the table and sniffed, inhaling any scent or perfume that might still linger on the cut pieces. He was attempting to discern any differences and he believed that he could. He tried to visualise those to whom they had once belonged. His hand slowly moved until it touched his groin and he smiled. "Behave! Work before pleasure," he muttered. The hair left on the other table was returned to the bag for disposal. It would be burned.

He collected a pair of domestic rubber gloves, a brush and a bowl of scarlet hair dye. The chosen strands were secured with a rubber band, dipped, then gently brushed before being placed onto a gauze, metal drying tray. Within the hour the samples would be dried, separated into batches and vacuum-sealed into small pouches. It was the second collection he had created. As before, half would go and half would remain in his care and so on this occasion, six would stay and six would be exhibited around the town. His early morning's work was complete.

He held the bags one by one to the sun's light and admired the scarlet strands as if it were an ancient ritual. He kissed each packet reverently mumbling, "Though your sins be as scarlet, they shall be as white as snow," before placing the twelve packets away in an octagonal *Quality Street* tin. As he pushed on the lid, he heard the sound of the door open and slam closed in another part of the building followed by footsteps crossing the room above him. He paused and closed his eyes. He knew the steps and he knew where they were heading. Within minutes another door banged followed by the deep, thumping bass. His peace had been destroyed.

Ignoring the noise, he moved towards a high shelf and viewed the line of wooden crosses collected throughout the county, long after their ceremonial placement; time and weather had aged them, now they were neither valued nor missed... They were perfect. He reached for a small hand drill. All in all he would plant thirteen.

Chapter Two

The PCSO looked at the damaged area and then sat on the bench next to Alex. He took careful notes as she described the youth in some detail.

"With the jacket, tear tattoo and face full of iron, we should be able to track him." The fact that Alex had mistaken the girl for a boy would prove to be the first hurdle the police would have to negotiate. He called it in to Control before standing and walking across the path to inspect the arched track of destroyed crocuses. He shook his head. "Pointless vandalism, I can never understand it."

Within the swathe of damaged flowers, the officer noticed a small, weather-beaten, wooden cross. The few remnants of the red petals from an artificial poppy still clung to the wooden intersection; the words *In Remembrance* were just visible through the grime and dirt. It was clear that it had been exposed to the weather for some time, partially buried and hidden within the spring flowers. He bent down, collected it and showed it to Alex. He noticed the small length of what appeared to be fishing line attached to the damaged base.

"It's been here some time by the state of it. Probably from the Cenotaph." He pointed down the pathway. "They'll leave nowt alone some of them, as you've seen today. Come on!" He finished writing his report on the smartphone and handed it to Alex. "Please read through that. It's a new system meant to save police time. We use it to upload reports and witness statements." He laughed. "When it works; we are dependent on a good signal."

She had not really been listening but scrolled down and read, nodding that the statement was correct before signing within the box on the screen with the attached plastic stylus.

7

"Looks nothing like my signature though." She smiled handing back the phone.

"Technology. I'll see you to the roadway and then put this back where it belongs." He held up the cross. "Are you sure you'll be all right?"

Alex smiled and nodded as she put the reference number he had jotted down for her into her bag.

He inspected the cross again and shook his head.

***

Cyril Bennett had crossed West Park after leaving the passageway that linked it with Robert Street. Although the sun was shining and the sky blue, the wind seemed cold as it funnelled through the gap between the buildings. Once across the road, its strength diminished. He glanced at the standing stone positioned to the side of the road, ring-fenced with iron railings, like the sole inmate of some bizarre prison. He remembered a sign that had been attached once which read, *Free the Harrogate One.* He chuckled to himself as he let his hand touch the rough-hewn sandstone. It marked the outer limit of the toll road in times past. Looking up, he noticed an officer in conversation with a lady on a bench. He thought nothing of it and quickly walked across The Stray heading for Otley Road and then on to the Police Station at Beckwith Head Road.

***

DS David Owen was already at his desk, a broadsheet spread across it hiding the detritus that normally lodged permanently on the flat surfaces that he called his own. A large Harrogate Festival mug contained a dark brown liquid that might have been tea but one could never be sure. It sat in a small pool of identical liquid. He glanced up as he saw Cyril approaching. Owen smiled.

Everyone called him Owen. When he was at police training there were a number of cadets in his year and so he was referred to as Owen and the sobriquet remained.

"Morning, sir."

Cyril returned the smile. "Still on the chilly side this morning, Owen."

"Your starter for ten, sir, this'll warm you. How many firkins in a kilderkin?"

He looked up at Cyril keeping his face straight whilst picking up the mug of tea. Droplets rained onto the paper and then his tie as the rim touched his lips. "Bloody hell, that's hot!" He quickly put down the mug, slopping more of the contents onto the desk.

Cyril smiled and shook his head. "Two. Half a barrel."

Owen looked at the paper and then at Cyril with an expression that conveyed his astonishment at his boss's knowledge. He nodded. "What about a hogshead?"

"Fifty-four gallons, Owen, or one and a half barrels' worth of Black Sheep ale. A butt is two barrels and a tun is equal to six barrels. Here's one for you. How many gallons in a tun?"

Owen hesitated, staring in admiration, taken aback by the sudden role reversal. He put his index finger to his lips to demonstrate that he was thinking... "My calculation... is... a lot."

"Two hundred and sixteen to be accurate. As you say, a lot. Why the interest?"

"It's in the paper here." Owen pointed to the article. "There's a local cooper who can't get an apprentice... sad really."

He looked down to read the relevant section to Cyril but watched as his boss turned quickly and moved to his office. Owen suddenly realised what he had done and he hung his head.

"Bloody hell... Cooper! I should have thought," he said as he screwed up the newspaper and tossed it into the bin. It hit the metal rim and the weight of the paper flicked the bin over, scattering the contents across the floor.

9

Cooper had been involved in the case that had seen their colleague, Liz Graydon, kidnapped and murdered. It was the small things that seemed to trigger Cyril's guilt... Owen might be clumsy but he certainly was not foolish... he would give him some time.

After fifteen minutes Owen knocked on Cyril's door and entered carrying a cup of tea. "Wasn't thinking, sir, brought you a brew. There's none slopped in the saucer neither."

"Thank you, Owen. Not your fault, it's fine. Sometimes it's as if the pin is driven into me, your memory can be your friend and then your enemy within a matter of moments. The word *cooper* always makes me think of Liz, as does Charles Horner." He forced a smile at Owen. "Maybe I should apply to be that guy's apprentice and make barrels, get out of this job, slip quietly away from the rat race altogether."

Charles Horner was a Victorian manufacturer of hatpins. Such a pin had been used to murder his colleague, DS Liz Graydon.

"You know what they say about old dogs and new tricks, Sir?" Owen turned quickly and left as Cyril's phone rang.

"Bennett."

Cyril listened, jotting down the occasional note. He sipped his tea and sat back glancing at the photograph of Liz that he kept in a simple, black frame on the top of the filing cabinet. When the call ended, he put down the phone, stood and crossed the room. It had been a while since they had had their usual one-sided conversation. Maybe like his counsellor had said, one day she would decide to just go, leave without warning and when she did, he must accept it. Maybe she had gone, moved on. He knew one thing for certain, he should move on too. He picked up the photo frame, moved back to his desk and slipped it in the bottom drawer as if putting the genie back into a lamp.

"I think it's time, Liz, it's time to move on. I know you'll always be near but not too near." He closed the drawer with a degree of reverence and left his office.

***

Owen was working on the computer when Cyril approached. He patted Owen on the shoulder, a gesture that assured Owen that his earlier thoughtlessness had been forgiven.

"Get your coat, we have a discovery near to Kent Lane, Ripon. Nature has opened up to us revealing items of great interest. Dr Pritchett is on her way. I'll explain in the car."

Chapter Three

Owen drove as usual. Cyril stared forward at the road and toyed with his electronic cigarette. He rolled it across his lips as if searching for inspiration whilst humming some indefinable tune. It was not until they were passing through Killinghall that he spoke.

"A sink hole has appeared overnight partially destroying and destabilising an old property and revealing what appears to be human remains; a large hole too."

Owen glanced sideways and then back at the road. "Regular occurrence in Ripon, I believe."

Cyril just raised his eyebrows. "Ripon's one of the most susceptible areas in the country for them owing to the Permian gypsum deposits. As to the extent and accuracy of the report, we'll have to wait and see."

"How's Dr Pritchett?" Owen glanced again and noticed a slight smile crack across Cyril's lips. Cyril and Julie Pritchett had developed a relationship that suited them both, neither wished to commit fully, both were married to their professions and so the casual nature of their affair was perfect. Initially it had started tongues wagging in the station but time had silenced the cynics.

"She's fine, Owen, and thanks for asking. Hannah?"
Owen simply grinned.

***

Kent Lane was closed with a tenuous, plastic tape strung between a fence post and a gate. The tape oscillated in the light breeze. Blue lights from the attending fire appliances competed with the bright spring sunshine. Cyril and Owen approached the tape and, after their ID had been checked, were escorted down the track to a further line of tape and some cones.

"Best not go beyond that, sir, not 'til we know the extent of the sinkhole. According to the Borough Surveyor, it could go right under the house and this track for all they know at the moment. It's being assessed further right now, that's the noise you can hear. They're using a drone, part of a new initiative with the CSI people, can you believe? Hear it? It's over there in the hole." He pointed in the direction of the sound, an obvious and unnecessary action that made Cyril bristle. "Utilities have isolated the gas and are working on the water now. Drains are damaged too, I guess, hence the aroma."

Cyril and Owen could make out the echoing sound of the drone's rotors, muffled by its concealed position. Owen, sensing Cyril's displeasure, quickly thanked the officer who moved back to the road.

"He was trying to be efficient, sir. Who's the Senior Investigation Officer?"

Cyril smiled. "Inspector Spence."

Cyril looked at the dirt ground under his feet and like a man about to walk on thin ice, gently tapped it with the sole of his highly polished shoe, before decisively taking a few steps backwards; only then did Owen see Cyril relax. He stared at the broken building. Taking the hint, Owen looked down before also quickly moving back.

The site was situated on the outskirts of the city, relatively close to the River Ure. The partially destroyed redbrick house made for a pitiful sight.

"Just look at it. It resembles a doll's house that's been opened to reveal the floor levels and furniture within."

Owen looked again at the ground and then at the building. Torn wallpaper flapped around the edge of the exposed lath and plaster internal walls as the lights swung, pendulum-like, from the ceilings. Pictures clung to the walls like drunken spectators, an upright piano was anything but as it leaned precariously on the very edge, uncertain as to whether it

13

was half in or out. Its final tune might well have been played. Water still poured from the fractured pipes, the tumbling streams allowing a partial rainbow to form as the sun caught its fall.

"Bloody hell!" Owen summed up the situation swiftly. "That would be some bloody alarm call in the middle of the night. Look how close the bed is to the edge. The gable end has disappeared into the hole. A quarter of the house has gone!"

"There's usually no warning, Owen, once the gypsum has been eroded it's just a matter of time, and the last few weeks of heavy rain have obviously triggered the subsidence. Luckily, only two people were in the house at the time and no injuries other than the couple being scared witless."

"The earth moved I bet for someone." Owen grinned and looked at Cyril, hoping to see a smile appear but received nothing, not even a flicker.

"Mr and Mrs Edge." Cyril turned to look at Owen. He knew full well he would think it a joke. "Edge, yes, I kid you not, so say nothing please, Owen. He's seventy-nine and she's a year older. Lived in the property since the seventies."

"So where are the human remains?"

"In the hole. What's strange is that they appear to be on top of and mixed with the masonry, so either they were in the house at the time of the collapse or disturbed from the sub-soil around the periphery of the hole during the collapse."

"So who spotted them?" Owen stood on his tiptoes as if trying to peer further into the distant hole.

"A Fire and Rescue Officer checked the house looking for the owner's dog and he spotted them when inspecting the cavity from the downstairs flooring. Initially he could not be sure as it was dark and he was using a powerful torch. However, he was wearing a helmet camera and on close inspection of the footage when he returned to the fire tender, it confirmed his original suspicion that generated the call to us and the pathologist."

"So is Dr Pritchett down there?"

Cyril pointed across the large field to a white and blue Tetra pop-up forensic tent.

"I believe that they're monitoring the images taken from the drone..." Cyril's voice carried a degree of incredulity, "... if I fully comprehend what our friend has just told us."

"The guy there's flying it," Owen interjected. "He's wearing video glasses so although he can't see the drone, he can see what the drone can see. It's probably sending images back to the tent as well as the lab. Bloody difficult to fly those things, I've tried. A number of forces are using them now as well as the emergency services; cheaper than a chopper."

"Really? I'll have to take your word for that." Cyril patiently smiled at Owen and raised an eyebrow; the technical information was of little interest. He felt an urge to ask Owen how it transmitted in real time but decided against receiving a long-winded explanation. All he was interested in was what they could discern from the images. "Well, if it's the only way an inspection can be carried out at present until the property and the ground is made safe, so be it. Come on!"

***

Inspector Spence greeted Cyril and ushered them into the tent. The HSE and Borough Surveyor were busy to the left of the shared trestle table, studying the geological charts. Julie Pritchett was standing next to Hannah Peters. They were both staring at a computer screen. Julie wore a single earpiece connected to a microphone and was directing the drone pilot to manoeuvre the craft to give the best possible images. She overheard Cyril's conversation and turned. She put her hand over the mic before calling them closer whilst pointing to the images on the screen. Cyril noted the eye contact between Owen and Hannah and was also aware of her slight blush.

"It's not easy to comprehend fully the circumstances," Julie explained. "You can see that there are a number of bones and bone fragments, also the remnants of items of clothing but

15

they appear to be separate and therefore may have no connection. You can see hair, possibly human but…"

Cyril leaned closer popping on his reading glasses. "That?" He pointed to part of the screen.

"Yes. What we can't understand from these images is what came from the house and what didn't. We'll only know when we can physically get in there."

Cyril turned and watched Owen disappearing towards the road, his mobile to his ear.

Julie continued. "Until it's been surveyed and made safe there's nothing to be done as there's no danger to life. There are severe fractures in the rear wall of the property and unstable ground to the right of the hole. We've been advised there is a likelihood of further collapse. If you want my immediate assessment, our person in the hole has been a long time dead so it would be unacceptable to risk further investigation until the site's been made safe."

Cyril put his hand on Julie's arm. "Thanks, Julie. Please keep me updated." He smiled at Hannah. "Hannah!" He turned to speak to Spence before following Owen to the road.

Chapter Four

The metal trowel cut the grass in a sawing, circular movement before a core of turf and soil to the depth of thirty centimetres was removed. It was carefully placed to the side of the new cavity. A small vacuum-sealed pouch was popped into the hole; a fine, transparent length of fishing line that had been connected to one corner was just visible as the soil was replaced. A large boot gently trod the turf making the recent work invisible. The *gardener*, still kneeling, leaned back and checked before threading the fishing line through a hole in the heavily stained wooden cross, tying it before forcing the cross fully into the ground, as if to mark the spot. He brought his fingertips to his lips, kissed them before touching the top of the cross. He stepped back, looked for a final time before lowering his head. Turning quickly, he walked clumsily from The Stray towards Tewit Well Road.

***

Owen was leaning against one of the tenders, chatting to the fire officers. Cyril walked towards them and Owen introduced him.

"This is DCI Bennett."

The officer put out his hand.

"Sir, just been chatting with Jim, here,"

Cyril shook Fire Officer Jim Yeats's extended hand and smiled.

"He snatched Mr and Mrs Edge from the property and then went back in to search for what they thought might be their missing dog."

17

"Is going in for a dog part of your normal safe operating practice, Jim?" Cyril asked, knowing what the answer would be.

Owen also turned to the fire officer.

"Usually, no, and the original assessment was purely to bring out the couple even though the building was in a dangerous condition, that's standard practice as you know. It was still dark when we arrived so using a drone was out of the question. Only owls fly in the dark." He turned smiling at Cyril and Owen but neither reciprocated. "If it had been light we'd have double-checked with our drone, it's equipped with a heat detecting camera. As I said, in the dark you've no chance."

"When I got to the bedroom, both occupants were very shaken. Mrs Edge was still in bed and afraid to move. Her husband, on the other hand, was wandering close to the side of the damaged floor. He was confused as you would be when part of your bedroom has disappeared in the middle of the night. It was difficult to see where the floor ended owing to the carpet being stretched over the void. He was obviously disorientated. He was calling for Ben. Even when I'd got them into the hands of the paramedics he was still asking for Ben so not knowing whether Ben was a person or a pet, we made the decision, after careful consideration, to do one final sweep. I went in once more but found nobody."

"So, you think that he could've been calling his dog?" Cyril enquired.

Jim looked at Cyril and then Owen, his facial expression changing. "Possibly but we couldn't be certain and we couldn't get any sense out of either so decisions had to be made to preserve life. We'd have looked bloody foolish if another incapacitated person had been in the house or even worse, in the hole!"

"Good point. I assume the couple have been taken to Harrogate?"

"Yes, as you'll know, shock can be a killer for people of their age."

Cyril held out his hand. "Thanks, Jim. If there's anything else you'll…" Cyril didn't finish as Jim interrupted.

"It's out of our hands now, it's all yours. A Scene Evidence Recovery Manager will be working under your guidance. HSE and the District Surveyor are on site."

Cyril smiled. "Seen them. Good job, Jim. Thank you!"

Owen and Cyril moved away. Owen spoke first.

"I called in and received details of the people registered at this address. Only the two living there, they've been in the house since 1968. Two kids, one male, Joseph, died in a motorcycle accident in 1979 and the other, daughter Emma Robson, lives at Barden Mill, that's…"

Seeing Cyril's frustrated expression, Owen did not finish his explanation.

"A69 between Haltwhistle and Hexham?" He did not wait for Owen to

answer. "Has she been informed?"

"In the process. I've asked that enquiries are made with the immediate neighbours regarding the possibility of a family dog."

Cyril nodded. "There's nothing else to be done here but you can check in on the couple when we get back to Harrogate." He fumbled in his pocket for his electronic cigarette.

***

Owen pulled onto Ripon Market Square close to the Obelisk. He parked near four red telephone boxes and an old, green, wooden cabman's shelter. Cyril jumped out and crossed to the butcher's, returning after five minutes carrying a paper bag. "Four Appleton's pork pies, Owen, a reward for our visit. They're still warm too."

The smell permeated the car, a delicious aroma of warm pastry that already had Owen salivating. Cyril placed the paper bag onto the floor by his feet.

"Well what are we waiting for?" Cyril looked at Owen who was staring at the bag. He sighed. "You are not eating one in the car, we'll sit on that bench."

Owen's demeanour changed as he leaned into the footwell and grabbed the bag. Within fifteen minutes, there was one pie remaining, secured in the glove box. Owen turned onto the ring road heading for Harrogate.

Chapter Five

The hospital was busy. Owen entered and waited until a space became available at the Reception desk. He showed his ID to the receptionist before mentioning the name Edge. She advised Owen to take a seat and informed him that someone would be with him shortly.

Within five minutes, a nurse in a dark blue uniform approached and introduced herself.

"DS Owen?"

Owen stood and smiled.

"We'll use this meeting room, Sergeant Owen, it's private." She lifted the watch attached to her uniform. "I can give you ten minutes, sorry."

It was unusual, as Owen only wanted to see and speak to either Mr or Mrs Edge or if a relative were visiting, they would do. He reluctantly followed. The room was typical NHS with the walls decorated with an upper and lower colour separated by a protective, wide, plastic dado rail. Two framed insipid looking prints were screwed to the wall; the light had bleached the colours to almost monochrome. The nurse sat and offered Owen a chair.

"Mr Edge passed away this morning and Mrs Edge has been sedated, the shock, it must have been so traumatic for them. They could both easily have died in that house. Heart attack, he had clear signs of heart failure."

Owen was not surprised after the description of events from the fire officer. "Did either say anything when they were brought in?" Owen leaned forward.

"According to the notes, Mrs Edge was asking after her husband. It was like a record constantly asking, *Is Ted here?* Clearly, she was severely troubled with Alzheimer's and to be

21

honest he was little different. All he would say was, *Ben, where's Ben, Ben's gone…* He would break down then become angry. The Doctor asked who Ben was but it was like talking to that television screen." She pointed to the flat screen television attached to the wall that was silently churning out medical advice.

"Was he just enquiring or was there more to it?"

The nurse looked puzzled by the question.

"Was he just asking or was he agitated, scared, anxious?"

"He was worried. He was constantly searching the room and asking anyone who came in. His mood changed from being upset to being quite verbally aggressive. He had to be restrained from getting out of bed on occasion but then as he was about to be sedated he had a massive myocardial infarction…"

"What about Mrs Edge?"

The nurse shook her head. "You'll struggle getting anything from her, she just keeps repeating, *Is Ted here?* Ted, you know, Mr Edge. That's all she's said. I'm amazed that they've remained in the house considering her physical and their mental condition. We're accessing her medical records but they are few and far between. Last visited her GP March 1979, I believe, a few weeks after her son was killed in a road accident. Motorbike. Nothing since then and Mr Edge has no record of ever being seen." Owen made a note to check the accident reports.

"You mentioned heart failure. Surely he went to be checked with that?"

"No, detected here when we wired him up. Severe too. His ankles were a right size, water retention, clear outward symptom."

"Has the daughter…" Owen glanced at the note he had scribbled on the back of his hand… "Emma Robson been in touch?"

"Nothing as yet, the only call has been from Jim, the fireman." She looked at Owen and then lifted her eyes to the roof in self-chastisement. "Sorry, let's be politically correct, the fire fighter who found them."

Owen thanked her and stood. He handed her his card and asked to be kept in touch with any progress. He also asked if she would keep mentioning the name, Ben, to Mrs Edge, in the hope that she might remember something.

As Owen left the hospital the sound of a siren could be heard somewhere in the distance. He quickly moved to his car. He leaned against it and watched the ambulance come to a standstill, the lights flashing blue. He rubbed his eyes before making a call to Control; he wanted the daughter's details. He needed clarification on a number of points.

***

As a member of the Major Crime Unit, cold case investigation was a small part of her role. DC Shakti Misra busied herself flicking through files she had removed from the two small towers that sat on her desk. It was a routine and orderly search. She occasionally turned to stare at the notes written on a whiteboard that stood on an easel at the far side of the room. She pulled her face, a contortion she had perfected since childhood when something just did not seem right. She tapped the pencil against her teeth before drawing a file from lower down the stack. Call it intuition but she had a feeling there was a key element waiting to be turned in an imaginary lock. Within minutes, her diligence had been rewarded, she heard the click in her head. "Bingo!"

Brian Smirthwaite walked past the end of her desk quietly whistling some unidentifiable tune. He paused.

"Cat got the cream I see by your face, Shak?"

"I've got a lead on Tracy Phillips, I think." There was a slight waver to her voice and her facial expression suggested that she might be presuming too much. "She's been missing for eighteen months... Look here and I'll explain. It'll help clarify my thinking too. Tell me what you make of this piece of information. Is it right or is someone playing silly games?"

Brian came around the desk and stood behind her.

***

Emma Robson nursed the coffee on her lap and stared around the interview suite. She stood and admired the framed picture on the wall and sipped her coffee. The door was ajar and she could hear the conversation interspersed with the occasional sound of laughter. It went quiet and only then did she reflect on the nature of her visit. She thought about her old home and then her mother whom she had just been to visit. The truth was, Emma felt nothing; there was no flutter of emotion but then neither were there any pangs of guilt. All the anger had gone. She had managed to bury the past. Quickly, she looked back at the picture.

"Mrs Robson?" Ruth followed Owen into the room. He smiled and held out his hand. "DS Owen and this is Ruth Jones, our Family Liaison Officer."

They sat informally and Owen opened the conversation by offering their condolences and quickly followed by asking after her mother. It was soon obvious that there was no love lost between them.

"Sergeant, let's not tread too softly on this. I'm here at your request and wouldn't have travelled down here of my own accord. I don't really know why I went to the hospital this morning, I guess to see if things might have changed." She raised her eyebrows and shook her head. "How may I help you?"

Owen outlined the discovery and the belief that the remains might have come from within the house. He was cautious as to what information was divulged.

"You know nothing of this family from what you say. First and foremost, I ran away when I was sixteen, pregnant and sixteen."

Ruth looked up from her note taking.

"You know that my parents were into the theatre, amateur stuff, pantomimes and plays initially. My father started directing too and enjoyed the power. He then managed to get more work professionally and things really grew quickly. The actors that you saw on the television started to come to our house. Everything suddenly revolved around plays and actors, in fact we, my brother and I, were co-opted at any opportunity. We both played Jesus in many nativities and then progressed. With the success came money and more fame. There were post-production parties too. They'd open your eyes; let's say that a number of eyes were turned away from some of the activities, the *lovies,* these thespians seemed to enjoy just that… love! I remember seeing my mother in bed with two male actors whilst my father would be elsewhere enjoying a similar activity."

"How old were you then?" Owen asked.

"Maybe thirteen."

"Your brother?"

"He, being older, enjoyed entertaining some of the more mature ladies."

"You?"

She paused and looked down. For the first time since the conversation had started, Owen sensed a degree of deep, emotional trauma.

"If you need a moment…"

She held up her hand, the open palm facing them, and then slowly raised her head. Owen noticed the tears.

"I was the Oscar, the prize, an award for the best actor, a reward award. It became expected. I got pregnant as I was approaching my sixteenth birthday. I was seeing a bloke who worked at the local farms. He was doing seasonal work. He seemed kind and gentle and he really didn't take me for granted. He saw me as Emma, a person in my own right and not an object, and we used to walk by the river. He made me laugh and feel special. He picked flowers from the fields and gave them to me. He cherished me, giving and not taking. Can you believe for the first time I had met someone I thought I could trust? I had never really experienced anything like that before. I remember when I told him my birthday was approaching he brought a lamb for me to hold and he said he would look after it and call it Emma. He brought me a present, a present just for me!"

Owen paused and let the words sink in knowing his next question might seem callous. "Was it his baby?"

Emma shook her head. "No. We never…" More tears appeared and she searched her bag for a tissue. "Sorry! I wanted to but he said no. He knew my age."

Owen looked at Ruth who moved and sat next to Emma slipping a re-assuring arm around her shoulders.

"Whose baby was it, Emma?" she asked.

Chapter Six

It had been three days since the Ripon visit and the Borough Engineers had worked tirelessly to secure the building. Netting, scaffolding and wooden buttresses formed a complicated splint that temporarily guaranteed the integrity of the remaining parts of the structure. The full extent of the sinkhole had also been determined and areas deemed susceptible to further subsidence taped off. A select forensic team had been cleared to work, extracting the human remains and potential evidence from the sinkhole.

Cyril stared at the screen and enlarged the images one after the other. It appeared that the Fire Officer had been correct in his assumption and the remains were human. What was significant was their condition; parts seemed to have been preserved, almost mummified, whilst other areas had decayed to the skeletal frame. The video images had been sent live and Cyril had watched with interest. He listened as the senior officer described the findings, identifying which parts could be immediately and safely extracted. It became clear that further excavation work would need to be done before more of the remains could be brought out. The video ceased. Cyril now focussed on the individual photographs that were being streamed.

It was one particular image from the many that attracted his attention, an image of a foot. It had been separated from the leg and lay isolated on the masonry. The taut, yellowish, transparent skin allowing the tendons and bones to show through, had the appearance of aged yellow cling film. What appeared most bizarre were the toenails. The vivid red nail varnish seemed totally incongruous yet affirmed the fact that these fragments were once human, were once alive. Cyril felt a

27

faint shiver run down to the nape of his neck. He flicked the next image quickly and stared at the partial skull. Although some dry flesh remained, there was no lower jaw and part of the right side of the left eye socket was missing; the jagged edges suggested some blunt trauma injury either pre or post mortem. He suddenly noticed the hair; it was positioned a short distance from the skull. He read the report attached to the image. He adjusted his glasses and stared at the hair again trying to comprehend what he had just read and to equate it with what he was seeing. His curiosity got the better of him and he typed the word *wig* into the search engine.

"Owen!" Cyril called whilst still reading the information on screen.

Owen trundled to the door, a half-eaten sausage roll between his fingers. Some fine flakes of pastry drifted to the carpet.

Cyril watched the cascading crumbs and sighed. "Have you seen these?" He pointed at the screen.

Owen approached the desk, looked briefly at the screen and nodded; his mouth full of sausage meat.

"What do you make of this one?" Cyril asked eagerly.

Owen positioned himself behind Cyril who quickly removed a tissue from a box and placed it onto the desk. He then pointed to the remains of the sausage roll in Owen's hand and then at the tissue as if directing traffic. Owen placed his breakfast as indicated. Cyril lowered his head as he heard Owen rubbing his hands together behind him. He could only imagine the number of minute, greasy crumbs that would now be either in his hair or on his shoulders.

"You can't plan for every eventuality, Owen!" he said almost to himself.

"Sorry?"

Had Cyril turned his head he would have noticed the faintest smile move across Owen's lips.

"Nothing, Owen. Nothing. You were going to say?" He brushed his shoulder with his hand as Owen spoke.

28

"Yes! I've seen the pictures from Ripon. Amazing how some parts of the body seem well preserved and other bits not. Could they be the remains of two separate people?"

Cyril turned and looked at his colleague with a raised eyebrow. To be honest, he had not immediately considered that. "A good thought, Owen, a good thought. Have you seen the foot? Gave me the shivers I can tell you. The hair also but according to the report it's a wig."

Owen leaned closer to the screen and expanded the image to focus purely on the hair. "Not read the report yet, just seen the pictures."

"If you look here," Cyril indicated, "you can just see the inside, seems like fine netting. I've just researched wigs and you wouldn't believe the complexity. They're referred to as cranial prostheses and the most expensive wigs are crafted from human hair. Were you aware that wigs constructed using Russian or virgin European hair cost a bloody fortune? There's all sorts from synthetic to cyber which is made from spun nylon..." Cyril heard Owen stifle a yawn.

"Not surprised they're expensive, not too many Russians or European virgins prepared to offer up their locks I guess!" As he spoke Owen looked down at the top of Cyril's head as if searching for signs of male pattern baldness before leaning over to pick up the remains of the sausage roll.

"A moment longer," Cyril instructed defensively whilst preventing Owen's hand from retrieving the food. "Contact Forensics and see if we're dealing with one or multiple remains and then see what you can discover about the hair. Find out if it's possible to trace the wig's owner from any distinguishing DNA or manufacturer's marks. Shouldn't be too difficult. By the way, I was interested to read your interview with Emma Robson, Owen. Who'd have thought that these things were going on there of all places?" Cyril mused with a naïvety that seemed contradictory to his years of experience.

"Don't forget the number of military bases in this area."

"She's definitely sure her father was the man responsible?"

"She is, but from the conversation we had, it could have been one of many. My money is on the kind boyfriend." Owen moved to the side of the desk.

Cyril simply smiled as he had thought the same. "Don't forget Forensics."

Owen leaned and collected the roll. "Not too difficult. I'll let them know you have full confidence in their abilities, sir." He left Cyril to scoop up the pastry flakes from his desk into the tissue.

"What news of the missing dog?" he called after Owen was out of sight, his question falling on deaf ears. He looked at the file on the computer detailing the results of the door-to-door enquiries. As far as the neighbours were concerned Mr and Mrs Edge had not had a dog for a number of years and it had not been called Ben.

He quickly read through the interview with Emma Robson again. She had refused to look at the photographs brought from the house. He noticed that a number contained famous faces from the past. Cyril paused at one of her brother on his motorcycle taken days before his untimely death.

***

Smirthwaite read through Shakti's notes. Tracy Phillips had last been seen leaving the hotel where she had finished her shift. She had been a room attendant at The Oak Hotel, having been appointed two years previously. Her work record was exemplary. She had always taken two days off midweek and worked weekends apart from on three occasions, one of which was the weekend before her disappearance. As far as her colleagues knew, she lived alone in a one-bedroom apartment off Cold Bath Road. Reading through reports made at the time of her disappearance, it seemed that neighbours rarely saw her and in two it appeared that the descriptions did not come close to matching. However, they did refer to her height. Both said that she was about six foot tall, described the cleanliness of the place and how quiet she was.

What both Shakti and Brian Smirthwaite had noticed from the evidence seen so far, was the distance she seemed to have created between herself, her neighbours and her colleagues; none seemed to know her well, even though they generally spoke positively about her. Her colleagues had nothing but praise for her work ethic and professionalism but none said that they really knew her. They had never socialised. Even at Christmas, she was either away or reluctant to become involved. She kept herself to herself.

Shakti read through the references received by the hotel when she applied for the job; they were exemplary. She was an enigma.

Brian flicked through a file. "Do we know if she's married? Kids?

"Divorced." Shakti held open the correct page.

"You'd think if she were as tall as they say that she'd have been spotted sooner. So what have you unearthed that's caught your attention?"

Shakti slid the photocopied note across the table and then sat back. "The original is with Forensics. Look at the date it was received." Her voice had an air of triumph but there was also an element of uncertainty.

Brian noted the date and read the three lines. He too then sat back and stared at Shakti. It was clear to her that he was assimilating what he had just read. There was a moment's silence. He read it out loud.

She's not gone anywhere.
She's just stopped walking these streets, a shadow of her former self… maybe… you just don't see… do you?

"It was found in a folded newspaper on a bench on Montpellier Hill yesterday and handed to an officer on foot

31

patrol. The finder was somewhat confused by the date and headline of the paper but discovering the note made him realise its importance, in fact, he was quite upset." Shakti slipped a photograph of the cover of the local newspaper across the table, the headline was clear. *Missing!* Followed by a photograph of Tracy Phillips.

"That's the first reporting of her disappearance! I remember it. We've had nothing since. Nobody saw anything, nobody's seen her, no relatives have come forward. It's as if she vanished off the face of the earth in a puff of dust. She's not named but it's a real teaser, it has to mean her."

"As I said, fiction or fact?" Shakti folded her arms. "The newspaper's in perfect condition, as if printed yesterday."

"What would we do without the support of the public in cases such as these?" Brian's words sounded sincere but the question as to the true identity of the person mentioned within the note was yet to be answered. It could have been interpreted another way. "Has someone been to see this…" he looked at the notes. "… Mr Baker, the chap responsible for handing it in?"

"Brought in to eliminate his prints from the paper and the note, he was accompanied by his daughter-in-law. She was well pissed off I can tell you. Kept going on to him about wasting police time. No CCTV facing the bench on which the newspaper was deposited and we're checking to determine whether the person who left it can be spotted on the other cameras in the area."

"What's to say your thoughtful member of the public isn't the guy who left it? After all it's not a straightforward case."

Shakti smiled. She had just landed that for which she had been fishing. "I think we'll pay him a visit."

***

Cyril turned off the computer and moved to a more comfortable chair at the far side of his office. He removed an envelope from his jacket pocket. It had been there since he had collected it from the mat on arriving home the previous day. His stomach fluttered as he brought the envelope up to his nose and sniffed gently like a sommelier with a classic wine trapped within the tastevin. He ran his fingers over the dark blue, handwritten script clearly stating that the letter was addressed to a Mr C V Bennett. The handwriting was beautiful, almost copperplate in style. Care had clearly been taken in the presentation, even the stamp was placed perfectly. He brought out a magnifying glass from the top drawer to look more carefully at the postmark. It was a smudge, impossible to decipher. His index finger was drawn back to the letter 'V'. The fluttering in the pit of his stomach now churned, an amalgam of uncertainty, anxiety and anticipation. Few people knew his full name; of those who did some had passed away and others knew better than to mention it. Cyril Vaughan Bennett. Cyril, he could live with but... Vaughan! He shook his head. Strangely, he knew from whom the letter had come and although it brought a degree of trepidation, it also brought a flush of uncertainty as his mind tumbled back too many years to a past he thought he had left behind for good. A violin's shrill notes suddenly played in his head, flushing it with memories of his childhood. He closed his eyes visualising the rise and fall of his mother's elbow as she bowed the violin's strings, and in his mind's eye he could see the lark ascending.

Chapter Seven

Brian observed the bungalow. The garden had recently received attention but it was purely cosmetic; it did not demonstrate the care of a dedicated gardener. Shakti rang the bell. Within a few minutes the door opened secured by a short chain and a face appeared in the gap.

"Mr Baker?"

The elderly man raised his eyebrows and then smiled.

Shakti held up her ID. "We rang you earlier to say we were coming. This is DC Brian Smirthwaite."

Shakti watched as Mr Baker propped both of his walking sticks by the door before it was closed and she heard the chain slip off the track. The door opened fully. Graham Baker collected his sticks and walked down the hallway. A stick in each hand steadied his slow progress. They passed two closed doors to the right. "This one." He directed with his left stick as if giving a road signal indicating his next faltering manoeuvre. He turned to see Smirthwaite close the door.

"No need for the chain. I'm sure that I'm secure with two of our finest in the house."

He entered the lounge and they both followed.

"Sit, sit. Sorry I took so long to get to the door, takes me an age to get out of my chair. I'd been watching for you too. Must've dozed off. Any luck with the newspaper?"

"You left a statement at the station about how you found the newspaper. Can you tell us again, please, Mr Baker?"

Smirthwaite took out his notepad and pencil.

"Ready?"

Graham Baker smiled and nodded. "Every Tuesday my daughter-in-law drops me off at the bottom end of St Mary's Walk and there's a bench I use whilst she does her shopping.

34

It's good to get out and watch the world go by. I don't get out enough, I'm told. Then we either go for lunch in one of the pubs or up to Betty's. However, this week I decided to take a little exercise. I had an accident a while back, damaged my spine. The reason for these." He half-heartedly waved the two sticks. "Anyway there's another seat just up Montpellier Hill, it's on the footpath facing the garden. There's a large, stone ornament, like a vase on a pedestal, full of spring flowers, you know the one I mean and I thought I'd sit there for a change. It's away from the road and quieter. The paper was there, tucked between the slats of the bench. I thought nothing of it, in fact, I was pleased to find it until I opened it and saw the headline and then the date. The note was inside. I got this shiver down my back, strange really. I remember putting it down as if it were going to bite. I saw a policeman and shouted for his attention. You know all of this."

"Did you see anyone leave the paper or watch you once you'd picked it up or see anyone move away when you called the police officer?"

Graham Baker shook his head. "My daughter-in-law said I was making a fuss and I should've just dropped it in the litter bin."

"We're grateful you didn't."

It was obvious that there was little else to glean from the conversation and Smirthwaite and Shakti insisted on seeing themselves out.

"Must have some kind of home help, bloody immaculate that house. A place for everything and everything in a place, made me think of Cyril," Smirthwaite said quietly as they made their way to the car. He was really thinking out loud.

"He has a wife according to the records. Didn't you read the full file that I handed you?"

Smirthwaite pulled a face. He knew that he had been a little excited by this latest information and he admonished himself inside for the slip. "Wonder why his wife doesn't go out with them?"

35

"Probably the daughter-in law takes him from under her feet, that's why the house is immaculate. Men tend to get in the way!" She turned and winked at her partner.

Graham Baker stood back from the window but watched through the net curtains until they had driven off. He turned and looked at the two walking sticks resting against the chair and smiled.

***

The brown terrier chased the ball thrown at some force and speed from the plastic ball launcher. Considering the size of The Stray and the extent of uninterrupted open space, the throw was poor as the ball crashed into the branches of a tree and ricocheted to the right. The dog stood momentarily confused but soon spotted the ball fall and roll to a standstill. It dashed the short distance, eager to collect its prey before suddenly stopping, more interested in the ground than the ball.

"Annie, fetch!" Barbara Doyle commanded. The dog, all wagging tail, continued to ignore the commands and the ball, it was far more interested in digging than retrieving. Barbara trudged across the grass. "Leave! What have you found now?"

Part of the turf had already been removed, flung backwards by frantic paws. Annie turned proudly revealing the small wooden cross that dangled from her mouth.

"Drop!"

The firm command had an immediate result. The terrier dropped the cross and ran to the ball. It was only then that the owner saw the plastic bag for the first time. She picked it up and the cross came with it swinging like a pendulum. When she identified the bag's contents she dropped it, more in confusion than revulsion. She was aware that some people practised strange rituals to commemorate the memory or the passing of a family member and thought Annie had disturbed such a memorial.

From the appearance and the condition of the wooden cross Barbara concluded that it had been there for some time. Had the dog retrieved the ball, it would still be secure, semi-hidden in the ground. She studied the tightly packed bag and confirmed that it was hair. She looked round but there was no one there other than a group of children kicking a football some distance away. Annie put down the ball and barked before backing away, keen to have it thrown. Picking up the cross, Barbara noticed that the black, plastic centre stud of what had once been the poppy was still attached and some lettering was still visible. It failed to make a word but she could guess, *Remembrance*. What was clear was the number '12' marked within a circle. She turned it over in her hand and the bag dangled like a transparent flat fish from the end of the line. Barbara was now confused and upset but out of respect she put the vacuum-sealed bag back into the ground along with the cross and reverently patted the soil and turf into place. She stood and for some reason lowered her head and whispered a quick, "Sorry." She backed away towards the excited dog.

Within minutes the ball was in the air and the dog was again in chase, this time well away from the disturbed soil.

***

Barbara had eaten nothing; she had only toyed with the food that was on her plate, moving it methodically from one side to the next. Her husband kept looking up at her. The dog, Annie, waited patiently in the expectation that her untouched meal would be transferred into her bowl.

"Penny for them. You've not been yourself since I came home. What's up?"

Barbara looked at Annie who immediately wagged her tail. Saliva dripped from her mouth in anticipation that food was soon to come her way. Barbara then looked back at Colin.

"Something strange happened today when we were out on The Stray. It's silly and probably nothing but I just can't seem to shift it from my mind."

Colin leaned across and covered her hand with his. "So what was it, love?"

She could see the worry on his face and smiled in the hope that it would lighten the mood. "Annie found it. Accident really. She dug up what appeared to be a memorial cross, you know the ones they plant at the Cenotaph on Armistice Day, the ones with the poppy attached. From the state of it I'd say it'd been there for a while although I've walked there many times and never seen it before."

"Could kids have removed it from one of the war memorials and dumped it there?"

Barbara shook her head and paused. "When I took it from Annie it was attached to a plastic bag by what looked like fishing line." She could see Colin's expression change as he was assimilating the information. "It was what was in the bag that made me uncomfortable..." She didn't wait for him to ask. "Red hair."

Colin squeezed her hand. "Are you sure?" His question was delivered slowly with a degree of doubt but he could see from her expression that it was true. "So what did you do with it?"

"I just thought that people have some strange ways of remembering a loved one who's passed away and that it was a small, personal memorial. Maybe it wasn't human hair maybe that of a dog or a cat. I don't know. Anyway, I felt uneasy so I just put it back."

"Have you mentioned it to anyone else?"

Barbara shook her head and started to cry. "Sorry it's me being stupid but if it were a memorial..."

"Bloody hell, love, it's something and nothing. It'll be kids messing about, nothing for you to get upset over. You've done nothing wrong." He came round the table and held her. Annie too sensed her distress and rubbed against her legs.

"Let's clear away and then take Annie out. You can take me to the spot. If it's kids it's probably gone by now. It'll put your mind at rest."

***

Barbara linked Colin's arm and he could sense her growing more reluctant as she approached the spot. Annie tugged on the lead.

"Look after the dog." Colin handed her the lead and moved over to the spot marked by the recently disturbed soil. He crouched and looked at the weather-beaten cross, protruding from the grass. He gingerly picked it up feeling the pull as the fishing line tugged at the buried bag. Moving the soil with his fingers he released the bag and stood, the cross in one hand and the bag in the other. He turned to look at Barbara and smiled in the hope of reassuring her that everything was fine. However, his gut told him a different story. He removed his mobile phone and dialled.

***

DC Stuart Park had finished the Sudoku and his coffee before he read the four reports that had been highlighted for his attention. At first they registered little, the only connections being the Remembrance crosses and the mention of a fine nylon not dissimilar to fishing line, connected to three identical sealed bags. The first report seemed purely incidental as it concerned a disturbance that had uncovered a small wooden cross not far from the town's main Cenotaph. The other three had been found in different locations, the last being the result of a direct call. Stuart looked at the images of the crosses and the transparent packets. There was a further forensic report pending on the bags' contents but he did have clear photographs showing the poor condition of the crosses and the numbers clearly written on them, 12, 1 and 13. Details of the two

39

specific location sites were included. Two more of the finds had been left at Craven Lodge, the town centre Police Office and another had been handed to a traffic warden so only a vague identification of these three locations was known. Stuart made a note of the caller's address before contacting the PCSO who had dealt with the disturbance that led to the discovery of the first cross.

Within the hour he was standing in front of the Cenotaph alongside PCSO Lee.

"This one, why the interest?"

Stuart lifted it from the ground with his gloved hand brushing off some loose soil to reveal the number 9. The thin line dangled from the base. He placed it in a plastic bag and sealed it.

"This is the fourth cross located this week; we have the other three. Did you find anything else below or near the cross when you discovered it?" Stuart asked.

"To be honest, didn't look. Is there something else?" The officer pulled a face. "Like what?"

"Can you show me where you found it?"

Within minutes, they had crossed the diagonal path on The Stray and were seated on the bench. "You can still see the swathe of damaged crocuses. Can leave nothing alone. Not managed to find the youth either. Probably low on the agenda."

Stuart slipped on another glove and gently lifted the soil following the curve where flowers had once grown. He saw the short remains of the fine line. Taking out his phone, he snapped a couple of images before turning the soil. There it was, the small plastic bag containing the scarlet hair. "Bingo!"

The PCSO looked at the object. Recalling his initial impression he laughed, believing now that it more resembled a dirty jellyfish. "Goodness me, I thought at first it was a condom!" He laughed again, staring more closely at the object but then as he discerned what was in the bag his demeanour changed.

"Is that what I think it is?" PCSO Lee peered at the packet.

"Human hair, scarlet, dyed, mixed human hair," Stuart emphasised.

"Right! I'll not dare ask." PCSO Lee simply shook his head. "The longer I do this job the fewer things surprise me."

***

On returning to the station, Stuart Park filed his report and checked that the latest find had been couriered for analysis. All he could do now was write it up into HOLMES and add the details to his whiteboard.

Chapter Eight

Cyril looked in the mirror and checked to make sure that he had missed nothing whilst shaving. He hated to see small areas of growth like those often left on Owen's face, through careless shaving. On some occasions they had been missed more than once and were extremely noticeable and distracting. Yes, he was fine. He tied the bow neatly, finally twisting it as it tightened and balanced. He then adjusted his shirt collar. If he had to wear a bow tie he was definitely not wearing one attached by elastic.

The reason he had accepted the invitation to a black-tie wine tasting he could not remember but Julie had been keen and so, probably when he was being distracted, a moment of emotional weakness, he had agreed. When he said *no problem,* the date had seemed so far off, but now, regrettably, it had arrived. He smiled when he thought of Julie but the smile slipped when his eye caught sight of the envelope resting on the mantelpiece. It remained unopened and he was determined that was how it would remain, for the time being at least. He slipped on his overcoat, flicked off the light and left the house; his mood had not been improved.

Cyril stood on Prospect Place by the front door of the hotel and inhaled the menthol vapour from his electronic cigarette; he relaxed and admired the view. The town's lights illuminated the road leaving The Stray, dark and mysterious beyond, delicately lit by the occasional old-style street lamp placed along the criss-crossing pathways. He turned to his right and looked down towards the town. At the bottom of the road the Cenotaph could be seen, illuminated by an ethereal, pale yellow light, in contrast to the dark sky. The taxi pulled up. Julie.

He smiled and opened the door. He heard her say to the driver *eleven* and his heart sank.

***

The noise emanated from the room at the bottom of the stairs that swept round to the left, the subdued lighting giving a warm ambience. Cyril handed their coats to an attendant and received a ticket. He slipped it into his wallet.

"Rare sight, my love!" Julie smiled. "It's all complimentary this evening."

She collected two flutes of English sparkling wine. "All the wines we'll sample are produced in England, even this." She touched Cyril's glass but could not fail to see the disappointment on his face. "You could have said no. Hannah would have come and certainly Owen."

"Pearls before swine giving this to Owen. Goodness, if it doesn't come in a pint glass and have a head on it he's lost. Besides it's a wine tasting not a wine glugging." He smiled. "I'm fine… uncomfortable talking English wine when I really know absolutely nothing about any of the vineyards."

"You'll be okay, stop worrying." She leaned across and kissed his cheek. She then wiped a trace of lipstick away with her finger.

They moved through a lounge and into the cellar area. Once through the glass doors, the passageways were cool and the lights dim. They were shown to a table. The notepad placed before them listed the wines. Apart from the glasses in the centre of the table Cyril noticed small jugs of water, plates of wafers and a spittoon. He made up his mind that he would not be using that.

The hum of excitement grew, echoing amongst the shelves holding the hotel's wine stock. The order and organisation of the event was beginning to suit Cyril; he was warming to the process. He watched how people held the wine to a light and swirled the contents in the glass, holding it by the stem before bringing it to their noses. He knew the process, he had read up on the Internet the dos and don'ts but still felt foolish trying to imitate their actions. He then saw them drink and perform some ritual of drawing air through their lips before holding up a spittoon.

***

The trowel cut the third hole of the evening. The sharp-bladed, curved edge made light work of it and soon the bag was lowered into the crevice, the cross was quickly tied to the line and the ritual was complete. The *gardener* brought his fingertips to his lips, kissed them before touching the cross. It would, he hoped, be for the last time. This was the final one he would leave, the ultimate offering. The others were now in situ, given out to await their fate; some buried, some exposed but all waiting to be discovered, some more easily than others. It would be God's will as to whether they would be found or left alone, handed in or simply thrown away. To the *gardener's* mind, those disposed of or left meant that they were given to the devil. The ones that remained with him had a more important role to play.

As if on cue the forecast rain started to drift in waves visible only in the streetlights and on the pavement. The droplets slowly filled and darkened the tarmac until tiny puddles began to form, each showing the myriad droplets' rings. He lifted his hood.

***

Julie was in deep conversation with a gentleman to her right about a red wine that she swirled around in her glass. Cyril read the bottle's label that it was a *Pinot Noir - early*. Cyril had had enough wine and conversation and was desperate for a vape. He excused himself and went up the stairs into the courtyard garden. He moved to shelter under a large garden umbrella, checked his watch, shook his wrist and looked again. A waiter came towards him holding a tray above his head.

"Time flies when you're having fun, sir," he said in all innocence. "May I get you anything?"

How wrong could perceptions be? Cyril thought but did not need asking twice.

Chapter Nine

Owen looked down at the table on which he had witnessed the autopsy of more complete cadavers. The human remains on this occasion were being ordered into the correct position by the diener to make what appeared to be the original form. Dr Julie Pritchett stood and assisted. Even to Owen's ill-informed eye, he could see that there were omissions. Dr Pritchett, hardly recognisable behind the safety visor and protective clothing, moved each piece with care but little reverence. Hannah looked up and smiled giving a small wave before photographing the objects. Owen listened to the conversation between the two women as they worked carefully and methodically. Julie paused, checking notes written on a pad at the head of the table.

"Morning, Owen. Drawn the short straw again, I note." She turned and smiled. "Male, early to mid-twenties. I know there's nail varnish on the toes," she said matter-of-factly. "It's my belief that our friend here was killed by a blow to the head; you can see the damage to this area here." She lifted the skull. "There's also evidence from toxicology of heavy heroin use. From what I see the body was dismembered shortly after death. The amputations are clean. That may answer the question as to why we see contradictions in the condition of the different body parts. There is still soft tissue attached to mummified skin and fibrous tissue present which has resisted putrefaction."

"So the body doesn't rot all at once?"

Julie smiled and paused before slowly turning to look at Owen. She was delighted that he asked questions; unlike Cyril, he showed a keen interest and had the ability to stomach an autopsy. She was more than happy to educate.

"In stages, Owen. Putrefactive changes occur in order but obviously depend on a number of circumstances." She pointed to her own body areas as she spoke. "Larynx and trachea followed by stomach, intestines and spleen followed by liver and lungs then the brain, heart, kidney, bladder then uterus. Amazingly, a virgin uterus lasts longer. The prostate putrefies at the same rate as the uterus, then the skin, muscle, tendon and finally the bone. That's the reason why we have this mixed evidence here."

Owen raised his hand as if in thanks.

"No problem, Owen, delighted that you take a keen interest." Julie returned to the table before looking back. Owen's hand was still in the air.

Bless him, he wants to ask a question or permission to use the toilet, she thought. "You have another question?"

"So we're looking at a murder?" Owen's tone sounded less confident as he lowered his hand.

Julie lifted the section of the skull. "You might make that assumption. I doubt he cut himself into pieces and then died."

Owen was unperturbed. "We know he was cut up post mortem but could he have overdosed and then fallen, the damage to the skull, or did someone give him a crack and apply..." He paused a moment trying to remember that French phrase Cyril had once used. "... the cut the grass? Can only remember the translation, sorry!"

Julie smiled. "That information cannot be discerned here and now. It will take much deeper investigation once we identify who this might be but right now my money is on the blow to the head."

***

Stuart Park scanned two separate reports, the forensic results from the hair samples and the DNA results received from The National DNA Database. The results were always returned directly to the force that had applied to the NDNAD. He had

47

badgered both parties for their swift analysis but the results from Forensics posed more questions than offered answers. The hair was a collection, a mix, made up from people of differing ethnic origin. According to the report, the scarlet colour was unprofessionally applied after it was cut. There was even a list of possible hair colour brands that matched the analysis. How they discovered these details was anyone's guess but he never questioned the accuracy of the findings. The results from NDNAD were a little more positive. Each packet, apart from one, showed no match to known stored DNA. He scanned down the page until he identified two names; one was a direct match whilst the other had been found using a familial search.

He printed details of both individuals and posted them onto a white board jotting down notes alongside. His mobile rang.

"DC Park." He listened as he studied the images of the crosses and the bags attached to the boards. "Two? Where? Have they been removed? okay. Right. You have full details of finders and the exact locations?" He grabbed a pencil and noted the information. "Thanks." He looked again at the board before moving to another part of the office. He popped his head round a partition. DC Harry Nixon was cleaning the fingernails of his right hand with a penknife.

"Busy?" Stuart said exaggerating the sarcasm in his voice.

Harry cleaned the blade on a tissue, folding it and slipping it into his desk drawer. "Depends on what you have in mind."

***

Cyril Bennett smiled as he studied the files from both cases and the words, *No shit, Sherlock* echoed in his head. It had not taken much nous to suggest that there might be a connection between the remains found within the sinkhole and the packets of hair found locally. Loose hair in packets and the discovery of a long-haired wig was too convenient and could only be a coincidence, he realised that, but it was not to be ignored. Neither the DNA nor the forensic details had been returned on the wig but he studied with interest the DNA results of the crosses and packets. It was as suspected; the crosses showed evidence that they had been weathered in different locations and made at different times. In one case the lettering and ink identified on it demonstrated that it was made pre 2001. For that year and subsequent years, the process had changed so accurate dating would prove impossible. However, considering the state of each cross it could be ascertained that they had been made a number of years ago and had been exposed to the damaging effects of the weather.

It was the familial DNA evidence that interested him. It was evident that hair from one person, trapped within the packet, was identified as a family member of Gideon Fletcher, a known petty criminal who had been arrested for GBH and racial offences between 2012 and 2014. After a short spell in custody, he had seemed to change. He was then better known in the town for dressing in the style of Jesus with long, brown hair, wearing only a rough, woollen tunic that went to his ankles. Cyril wrote a note *Chiton of the Lord*. That information had been dredged from some dark recess of his mind but where he had first heard the term he was unsure. Gideon also wore sandals with no socks and always carried a small banner stating, 'Jesus lives. Sinners repent.' No matter what the season or what the weather he could be seen, wearing no other protective clothing, wandering and waving to anyone he saw around Harrogate. He was always ready with a smile. Not only was he a regular around the spa town but he was also known to walk miles, handing out pages from the Bible he stashed in a small canvas satchel. He was often seen in Masham, York, Knaresborough and Ripon. It seemed the sinner had somehow become the saint. People would give him food and shelter. He was genuinely liked.

Cyril read through the report. His last known sighting was on January thirtieth, 2016. The vicar of St John's, Clipton, had found him leaning against the Telfer Pyramid Grave in the churchyard. It had been snowing and he had noticed the tracks leading between the gravestones and had followed, finding Gideon. He initially led him into the church before taking him home. The report detailed that he was fed and offered a bed for the night but he had demurred and had even turned down the gift of an overcoat. It was about nine p.m. when he left. Gideon had informed the vicar that he had family locally and would go there for a day or two.

Cyril rolled the mouthpiece of the electronic cigarette between his lips whilst scribbling some notes, enjoying the cool, menthol taste on his tongue.

The last known sighting January 2016. Cold night, inappropriate clothing. Telfer Pyramid Grave (significant? What? Who?) Check for nearest family member.

Speak with Reverend Ian Fella.

He underlined the last sentence before looking at the only photograph they had on file of Gideon after his *Road to Damascus* moment. The old press cutting showed clearly the weather-beaten, grinning face. Cyril smiled at the plaited rope tied around the loose chiton, the one-piece garment. He carried no possessions other than a small, homemade banner and canvas satchel.

Cyril noted that the results from the tests showed only that the mitochondrial DNA demonstrated a maternal connection and so the owner of the hair samples could be Gideon's own mother or one of his siblings. It ruled out the chance of belonging to any offspring he might have had. Cyril looked at Gideon's mug shot taken in 2013 and compared the two images before attaching them to the white board and adding the notes *saint* and *sinner* beneath the relevant images. All Cyril had to do was to track Gideon's family and that should not prove difficult. He made the necessary call. The tedious task was set in motion. The simple questions of by whom and for what reason they were buried might take a little longer to solve.

***

Stuart Park and Harry Nixon looked at the two objects that were trapped securely within protective, plastic bags; each was labelled with the information concerning finder and location. Park turned them over in his hands.

"Every one is numbered, on this one it's scratched into the surface of the wood. This one, some kind of marker pen."

Nixon picked one up and studied it. "Look bloody ancient, both of them. How long have they been dumped? Is that what I think it is in the bag?" He looked at Park, his face contorted by the quizzical expression.

"Human hair, dyed scarlet and not all belonging to the same person. However, these are not the first found. See, as I said, each is numbered. So far we have 1, 9,12, 13 and now we have 8 and 6," Stuart Park said with a degree of confidence.

"Meaning?"

"Haven't the foggiest. That's what we're here for. Could be someone buggering about and then again, it could be significant. Who knows what we might find next. Remember the jars of honey in that case last year? The clues made no sense at all until *Flash* came up with his theory? Well. Watch this space!"

DCI Cyril Bennett had acquired the nickname, *Flash*, early in his career. It was incorrectly believed that it was because of his neat and immaculate dress sense but that was far from the case. Initially he had been nicknamed *Gordon* after the wealthy benefactor of and lover of all things fast, initiating the Gordon Bennett Motor Racing Trophy, but then someone changed that to Flash Gordon, which then was shortened to *Flash*. It would be a brave acquaintance who would use this moniker now however.

Both officers went to the locations where the crosses had been found and inspected the immediate area for anything of significance. Nixon decided to take images of landmarks that could be seen from the locations. They were placed or buried for a reason, and anything that might shed light on that was worth pursuing.

***

Within the hour, each officer had interviewed the finders and was heading back to the police station on Beckwith Head Road. They now needed to prepare everything for the briefing planned for early the following day. Both were ready for home.

Chapter Ten

The rain had stopped temporarily but the sound of the occasional passing car splashed through the puddle-covered road. The Volvo estate was parked and the driver checked the rear-view mirror. He dropped the glove box lid and ensured that the tablets and the condoms were there. A programme from the Asian network played on the radio. He strummed along on the steering wheel, occasionally glancing at his watch. He had been assured that she would come and that she would be young.

Within minutes he spotted her in the wing mirror. She was smoking a cigarette as she approached while checking the parked cars that lined the roadside. He leaned across and opened the passenger door.

She took one long drag on the cigarette and dropped it in the gutter before climbing in. He opened his window to let the cigarette fumes dissipate, started the car and pulled away from the curb. Nothing was said.

His hand had slid across and grabbed her inner thigh. She moved it.

"Fuck off, not until I get the stuff."

A car pulled out within seconds and followed.

***

Cyril sat with his feet up. He pondered the events of the day before being distracted by the small oil painting illuminated by a spotlight. It was a felt pen sketch of a line of flat-capped gents, each with their heads down and their hands searching their pockets. It was titled, 'It's not in my Pocket' by the artist John Thompson. Cyril smiled thinking it resembled a group of coppers searching for a missing clue. He stood, studying it more closely and then switched off the light. He had a briefing first thing, and so an early night beckoned.

***

Within twenty minutes the car pulled onto the remote lay-by. The rain was now driving, almost horizontal. There was a slight glow of distant lights but nothing else. Rain ran in streams down the windscreen and the car rocked slightly when the wind blew.

"What's in your mouth?" he quizzed.

She stuck out her tongue revealing two gold studs sitting there.

He raised his eyebrows.

"Interesting! Back seat now or it's a fucking long walk back home for you."

He leaned into the glove box and grabbed the items before dashing to the back door. She also moved quickly. She took the tablets he offered and the two twenty-pound notes as he fumbled with his trousers.

"How old are you?"

"Why do you give a shit?" She grabbed his hand and thrust it between her legs. "This old. Is that old enough?"

He laughed excitedly. "You're the same age as my daughter. I'd kill a man who did this to her."

"Whatever."

His strong breath made her move away slightly and turn her head to the side avoiding his attempt at a kiss. The noise of the rain hitting the car's roof stopped briefly as the downpour eased momentarily. She watched as he fumbled with the condom. "I need a piss. All this water! A minute."

She opened the door.

He grabbed her arm and squeezed, noticing her wince. It hurt. "Hurry up!"

He watched her dark shape barely silhouetted against the night sky as she moved and squatted round the front of the car. He could neither see her move away nor the smile that was on her face. The rain started to thump on the roof again. He looked to the front of the car but saw only the faint flicker of lights in the murk, further blurred by the rain-streaked windscreen.

Moments later and to his relief, the car door opened. "About bloody time…"

The interior light came on and to the person looking in it was clear that the man inside was naked from the waist down. The light spilled out onto the figure that was crouching and staring in, his focus clearly on Kumar.

"What the fuck… Who are…?"

The rear seat passenger peered at the masked face staring back. He was unable to make out any facial features of the figure positioned by the open door. He was confused and embarrassed. Torchlight suddenly blinded him. His hand went up to shade his eyes and his other hand went to cover his exposed genitals. The memory of the masked face looking back at him would be the last thing he would see apart from the blinding light.

"Mr Kumar, number three. How delightful to make your acquaintance." The words were clear and precise and that enunciation brought with it fear.

Kumar, once he had fully comprehended what was said and what was happening, was about to protest again but the unseen, first flush of fluid had hit him squarely in the face. His vision suddenly blurred and turned a yellow opaque as the acid started to destroy his eyes. It filled his mouth, numbing and swelling his tongue. What suddenly became apparent was the smell, the smell he could not identify but in fact was the stench of melting flesh. All that could be heard was a gurgled scream as his face and tongue began to burn, blister and melt. The rain on the roof had been drowned out. As the first liquid burned, his hand frantically rubbed his eyes trying to clear away the liquid but to no avail, they too simply began to slough and blister. The pain was so intense that he did not feel the second liquid strike as it was poured specifically over his exposed genitals and thighs. It would be the final act against Kumar; it was all that would be needed.

Casually, as Kumar writhed in the back of the car, the attacker replaced the lid on the container; it would be tossed into bracken a few miles from the site, and with luck never found. He opened the front door to the car and attached a plait of hair to the rear-view mirror.

The frenetic thrashing of the body in the back seat continued for a few moments and suddenly, as if a switch had been flicked, Kumar's upper body slumped onto the rear seat, his face now unrecognisable. There was an occasional twitch and spasm but nothing more.

"Goodbye Mr Kumar."

The attacker closed the front door and walked back to the tree, removing his mask as he went. The cool night air and occasional slap of rain brought relief. He took a deep breath.

Chapter Eleven

The briefing room was busy. The large, blue screen emblazoned with the North Yorkshire Police Crest glowed proudly and the chatter was loud. Cyril lifted his cup from the saucer and scanned the room before sipping his tea. It was at moments like this that he missed Liz, her energy and enthusiasm. He looked across at a new face and smiled. He could see from her body language that she was nervous. Owen came in last carrying his customary Harrogate Festival mug. It appeared to leak as usual. He also carried a small cardboard box.

Cyril checked his watch, shook it and then looked again. A number of the room's occupants smiled. The meeting was about to commence.

"Morning all. I'd first like to introduce formally our new colleague, DC April Richmond. She's moved from Leeds on a temporary posting, recommended highly by DI Claire. I'm sure you'll all show your usual professional support." He smiled again at her and noted her colour rising. He also saw Shakti put her hand on her shoulder. He continued. "If you need anything, anything at all, just ask, we work as a team. Stuart will take us through the first element of today's briefing."

Stuart Park flicked the screen's remote and the blue-crested image faded to be replaced by a shot of a wooden cross and the attached plastic bag. He went through the findings and details about the DNA links.

"We have a connection with a Gideon Fletcher but also a problem as he's been off the scene for a good period of time. Fletcher was a bit of a handful at one time. He was a well-built six foot four and a right bastard, particularly when it came to race relations and in that area he had only one agenda. It was believed that he was behind a number of incidents involving people who, for want of a better phrase, were of a different colour, ethnic background or religion. When the terrorism activities with ISIL started to flood the news, we noticed a spike in the number of attacks on Asian and Muslim businesses. It seemed that any Muslim was fair game. Vandalism of cars, taxis in particular, shops and even abuse of people walking the streets. He's also smart. We believe that he encouraged the local youth, through the distribution of drugs, to carry out some of his dirty work. However, he was arrested and sentenced to eighteen months for ABH and racist abuse, early 2013. On release from prison he was a changed man."

Stuart posted the image of him in sackcloth and sandals and went through the details. "Completely changed character. Last known sighting was in January 2016. Extensive searches and missing person advertising found nothing. Simply disappeared. He's still on the North Yorkshire Police missing persons site."

"What about the numbers on the crosses?" Owen asked whilst jotting down the numbers displayed on the screen.

"What you see, just random. Whether there's any significance we – "

Cyril interrupted. "Open mind everyone. They're not there for fun. If you look, some are written and this one is scratched into the wood's surface. As I say, keep an open mind."

April Richmond scribbled notes frantically.

Park continued. "I have an appointment to see the vicar at St John's. He was the last man to see Gideon."

"Owen?" Cyril looked at Owen who put down his mug, wiped his mouth on his sleeve and took the remote.

Seeing the wipe, Cyril just shook his head.

"First thing, news from the hospital. Mrs Edge died today. Pneumonia." Owen paused. "However, we now know that they didn't have a dog, just a corpse in the house. The remains found in the sinkhole at Ripon are those of Matthew Benjamin Boffey, originally from Hawes. Records show that he was twenty-two when he went missing. Now here's the interesting bit. The pathologist suggests that the post mortem results show the approximate age of death as older by ten years but it's not an exact science."

Cyril raised his hand, indicating that he wanted to interject.

"Like our missing Gideon, Boffey was here one day and gone the next. Despite an expansive search he was never traced until now. Boffey has no relatives living in the UK, only an elderly aunt who lives in Australia. She's in a care home and can offer little assistance. The original interviews are in file 6b in your folders. Carry on, Owen."

"Body was sectioned after death and we believe the death was by a blow to the head. Evidence of heroin traced within the skin sample but not within the bone samples which suggests not a long-term addict. There's an open question as to whether it was self-administered or injected by someone else. There's also a question mark about the quality of the drug." He paused, leaned over and drank from his mug, again cleaning his lips on his sleeve.

"When will the toxicology results be completed, Owen?" Shakti asked as she moved a chair next to April and glanced at the copious notes that April had made. "And how do we determine if he or someone else administered the drug?"

"As soon as, that's all they'll say. We need to find someone who knew Boffey to determine whether he was a drug user."

"Now I need to discuss the wig." Various images of the hairpiece taken at different angles revealed little to those within the room. "File 7a. We received permission to take DNA samples from Mr and Mrs Edge and the daughter co-operated too. We have a match for all including Mr Edge and Boffey." Owen turned and looked at Cyril whose return glance said, *tell more.*

"Skin and hair within the fabric weave. We know the wig is not human hair but a synthetic nylon popular in the sixties and seventies. The label..." he flicked to the correct photograph "...the company no longer exists. It has been suggested that it might have been used in some theatrical productions, consequently the number of DNA sample matches. From interviewing the daughter, both parents were thespians, so possibly make up and wigs might have been stored at the property."

Owen flicked through a few family photographs of them dressed for a production of Aladdin and then the signed photographs of TV and film actors popular at the time.

Owen looked up. "File 8. Please look and read."

There was a silence as many read again through the interview with Emma Robson. It was Cyril's turn to speak and he brought the briefing to a close.

"As you can see there is a suggestion of incest and that her father had insisted on the termination. It was as a consequence of this that she left. Sadly, the man responsible is dead. The first thing is to see if Boffey, the body in the hole, is the boyfriend. If that turns out to be the case, we can assume that she'll know whether he was a drug user. My hunch is that she told him first that she was pregnant and who the father was. What happened after that may never be determined. Owen and Ruth are meeting with her tomorrow with a photograph we have of him from when he went missing. We know he did farm work but whether they are one and the same...? Maybe by tomorrow we might have answers to a few more questions."

***

Cyril stood in the corridor leaning against the wall. It was cooler and he closed his eyes for a moment. He could feel the headache starting between his eyes and he began to rub the spot. Shakti came past and tapped his elbow gently.

"Sorry, but you might want to ask April Richmond about the notes she made during the briefing." Shakti smiled and turned to follow Owen.

Cyril smiled and thanked her before re-entering the briefing room. April was looking at her phone and then the whiteboards focussing particularly on the images of the crosses.

"Any ideas?" Cyril's voice startled her.

"Made me jump, sir." She collected her notes. "It's probably nothing but the numbers on the crosses. You said to keep an open mind but, I'm afraid I couldn't stop thinking about something I learned when I was a student. I teach teenagers in my Sunday school class, and the other week we were talking about numbers connected within religions, in particular Christianity."

"Sit down, April. Please talk to me."

She paused and looked a little apprehensive before opening her notebook. "Let me just say that listening to DS Owen talk about the significant change in the man's demeanour and character made me think of the crosses and hair and the way that they were left. Whether it was the intention that they be found, I can't say, but I was fascinated by the way whoever did this had separated the cross from the other element, the bag containing the hair. One was buried, gone, invisible as if in the past, and the cross, the symbol of Christ, was above it and left prominent. These are only my thoughts, sir."

Cyril smiled and nodded. "I understand. Go on, please."

"The hair, dyed scarlet, possibly for the devil or evil. I know it's hazy and I'm not too sure yet with my ideas on that. I'll have to give it a good deal more thought. I see a connection but it's tenuous."

Cyril saw the light immediately and nodded. "And the numbers?"

"Sorry, yes. Getting ahead of myself. One of my problems. You know that certain numbers are associated with Christianity, thirteen is quite well known, thirteen people at the Last Supper, thirteen is symbolic of rebellion and lawlessness, thirteen, the dragon or Satan. Let's not forget that Nimrod, who tried to take God's place was thirteenth in Ham's line according to Genesis 10.9. Don't worry, I looked it up straight after the

61

briefing along with this…" She turned her notebook round for Cyril to read the notes she had made.

Mark 7:20-23
Jesus mentions thirteen things that defile a person: For from within, out of the heart of men, proceed evil thoughts, adulteries, fornications, murders, thefts, covetousness, wickedness, deceit, lasciviousness, an evil eye, blasphemy, pride, foolishness: All these evil things come from within and defile the man.

Cyril looked at her and then at the notes on the whiteboard, focussing on the numbers. He raised an eyebrow.

"Interesting. Be ready in half an hour, you can come with me to interview the last man to see Gideon Fletcher before he vanished and you might speak his language." Cyril tapped the notes with his finger. "Half an hour."

Chapter Twelve

Shakti looked at the three names, Gideon Fletcher, Matthew Benjamin Boffey and Tracy Phillips. All missing. All had simply vanished and despite extensive searches and use of local and national appeals to the public for information, there had been nothing until the discovery of Matthew Boffey's body.

"So where are you now, Tracy? *You don't walk these streets but you're a shadow of your former self.*" Shakti wrote on a piece of paper twice as if searching for inspiration. "Why no longer walking? Why a shadow? How has she changed? You walk, so you are alive and if your hair was matched to the sample found recently then you are still here, unless of course the hair was taken from your body at some time in the past."

Shakti checked to see if the notification sent to every hairdresser had returned any results but there was nothing. The social media posts had brought the usual timewasters but there was nothing positive.

***

Owen checked his speed as he by-passed Haydon Bridge on the A69.

"Just coming up on the left." It had taken a couple of hours to drive from Harrogate.

Ruth Jones put down her book and stretched in her seat. She collected her note pad and checked her notes for the fourth time.

"It's always better chatting on their home soil, Owen. With luck we should glean a good deal." She checked the photograph of Boffey used during the public appeal when he had gone missing. She smiled at the fashion of the day.

"Wonder if Cyril wore a suit like that?" She turned the picture towards Owen who smiled. "Probably still has it."

***

Cyril was happy to let DC April Richmond drive. He listened as she told him more about her career to-date.

"I spoke with Reverend Ian Fella this morning and he's expecting us just after ten. We're meeting at the church. He's going to walk us round and let us see where he met Gideon."

"This might sound like a silly question but are we alert to the fact that the Gideon's Bible is left and given to people in a way that Gideon gave out pages of the Bible?"

Normally Cyril would have been annoyed at someone stating the obvious but he simply smiled. The car pulled up by the church gate.

He slipped on his coat; the wind blew from the river and along Bondgate Lane, bringing a noticeable contrast in temperature to the warmth of the car. The small, ornate gate to the church was closed. Cyril paused for a moment to admire the castellated, stone tower and the composition of the architecture. Some large yew trees of indeterminable age stood to the right along the boundary wall. He opened the gate allowing April to enter. She followed the slightly curving path between the gravestones to the church door. Cyril tried the door and like all churches, the air seemed to rush past as it swung inwards. The peace was palpable.

"Is that you DCI Bennett?" a voice echoed through the nave.

The Reverend Ian Fella appeared from one of two arches that edged the chancel. Seeing April sitting with a bowed head, he paused momentarily and smiled.

Cyril introduced DC Richmond. Ian Fella shook her hand and then turned to Cyril. The handshake was gentle.

"Thank you for seeing us."

"More than happy to help. Let's go and I'll show you where I met Gideon and then we'll go through to the vestry, it's warmer." He smiled and turned. "This way!"

April looked at Bennett who simply smiled and allowed her to follow first.

The pyramid grave was just that. Cyril photographed it as April noted the vicar's comments.

"It's hard to believe it's spring. Let's go back in."

The vestry was significantly warmer. An electric radiator was positioned near the large desk. Ian Fella allowed his hands to hover just above it. "When will this spell of wet weather leave? Goodness, the older I get the more I feel the cold." He held a chair for April and then found his own.

Cyril opened the interview. "What exactly do you remember of that January afternoon?"

"I've been giving it quite a lot of thought since your call. You know about finding him by the pyramid grave. You know a little of biblical Gideon, Detective Chief Inspector, yes?"

Cyril looked at April and nodded. He did not, but he knew someone who did.

The Reverend continued. "Gideon was likened to Moses; he was directed like Moses who freed his people from the Egyptians so Gideon freed them from the Midianites. It was the first time I saw the connection."

Cyril felt as though he were way out of his depth and when he saw April nodding and taking notes, he knew that he had to bring the interview back on track. "So why did he say that he was here on such a cold evening?"

"He didn't and I didn't ask. He was standing looking at the pyramid grave. He said he came as often as he could. It was where God spoke to him, corrected, yes, that's what he said, *corrected him*."

"What happened then?"

"We came into the church and I gave him a drink from my thermos flask. I invited him home for a hot meal and I'm pleased to say that he accepted but after that he assured me

65

that he had to leave. He said that he had family locally and they would give him shelter. He even refused a coat that I offered and mumbled something about an ephod. That shocked me. His mood changed at that point and he left."

It was Cyril's inquisitive look that brought April to his rescue.

"An ephod is a priest's garment. Gideon made one from collected gold and made his people worship it. He lost his religion, became apostate as did Moses."

Cyril smiled, he was still lost in the wilderness of theological confusion and he wanted to get the interview back to the level where he had some understanding. "So he left and you never saw him again, not even by the pyramid?"

"Detective Chief Inspector, we get several visitors to the pyramid for many reasons but as far as I'm aware, the man of whom we now speak, has not returned."

"Thank you for seeing us." Cyril smiled. "During your time together did he mention his past? Did he talk about numbers?"

The vicar shook his head. "Sorry!"

Cyril stood and put out his hand. "Thank you for your time."

They moved back through the church to the porch.

"I don't know if this is anything but he gave me a page from his satchel. It was from Isaiah 1:18, around which he had tied a scarlet thread."

April spoke immediately, "Though your sins be as scarlet, they shall be as white as snow; though they be red like crimson, they shall be as wool."

The vicar quickly turned and looked at April, astonished by her biblical knowledge. He rested his hand on her shoulder. "Bless you, yes, that very passage. It is what he said afterwards that made me slightly uncomfortable."

"And what was that?" Cyril asked as his phone rang. He dug it from his pocket holding up a finger.

"Bennett. Where? You know the procedure. Forty minutes." He slipped the phone back into his pocket. "Thank you very much. We have to dash. Emergency call."

"Do you wish to hear what he said that made me uncomfortable?"

Cyril turned with a look of impatience written clearly on his face.

"These were his parting words:

Like Rahab, all Christians have a scarlet cord hanging in the window of their soul. As he got to my gate he stopped and turned to look at me directly and then said, *Including you."*

"What was he insinuating?" Cyril's expression was now one of total curiosity.

The vicar simply spread his arms. "We are all guilty of sin, Chief Inspector."

"Do you still have the page and the thread that he gave you?"

The vicar smiled. "I couldn't destroy it and I couldn't keep it at home. It is safely kept here. I'll be happy to see it go." He moved through to the vestry and returned with a small envelope.

***

The farmhouse was large, chickens moved along the hedge scratching and pecking as a dog barked from somewhere nearby. The door to the barn opened and Emma Robson looked out. She checked her watch.

"DS Owen and Ruth. You're earlier than I thought; usually the traffic is bad on the A1 at this time. You'll be ready for a coffee." She moved across the yard and slipped off her boots before entering the house. Ruth and Owen followed.

They sat round the kitchen table; the coffee and warmth from the Aga was welcome. A border collie walked in, looked at the visitors and left.

"We've brought a photograph of the missing man. We now know his identity. He disappeared about the time you left home. We'd like you to take a look and tell us if it's the man you knew."

Ruth looked at Emma first to make sure that she was up to it before she slid the folder over to her. Both she and Owen watched for her initial response. They immediately knew that they had found their missing man.

Chapter Thirteen

The body was still in the position in which it was found. Brimham Rocks Road had been closed at the junction to the entrance of the National Trust site. The Crime Scene vehicles had parked on the road leaving the crime scene open. Within thirty minutes Cyril pulled up at the police cordon. He showed his ID and the barrier was removed. He was directed further up to the second tape and the cars parked to the left of the road. The sky had been threatening rain all morning and now he was exposed on Brimham Moor, he could see in the distance the approaching curtain of wet weather. He grabbed an umbrella from the car. April Richmond followed him turning up the collar on her coat.

"What do we have?" Cyril looked at the officer standing by the tape who glanced at Cyril's ID.

"Sir, ma'am. One body. Male, Asian. Found earlier this morning. A van driver pulled in to the layby for a pee and found himself staring at what was once a human being in the back of an estate car. Immediately called 999. Luckily for him he didn't go near."

"What time was this?"

"08.20 I believe. The weather was atrocious last night. There'd be few sightseers around at that time when the rain was so bad. This area is known as a spot for lovers. There's the car parks used by people visiting the rocks just down the road but they're closed at sundown."

"A gate?"

"Yes. It was too convenient and too private. Problems with 'dogging' in the past." He raised his eyebrows. "Takes all kinds to make a world, sir."

"Indeed. Pathologist?"

"Chemical emergency called so nobody could go into the area until it was deemed safe. I believe it's an awful mess. Some kind of acid they said. Frosted the glass where it hit so you can imagine what it did to anything else in its path."

"Pathologist?" Cyril asked again hoping to achieve a simple answer.

"Dr Pritchett."

Cyril smiled inwardly. "May we?"

The tape was lifted and they moved to the side where he could clearly observe the crime scene. The car could not be seen. It was parked within what looked like a large, inflatable, blue and white Forensic tent. The hum of a generator keeping the tent inflated droned constantly. The Crime Scene Manager approached. He smiled as the rain started to drive directly at them. He pointed to a car and they quickly made a dash.

"Looking at the evidence collected from the area around the car, the theory to date is that one or more persons attacked the victim. The rear window was shattered from the outside and he has suffered very serious acid burns to the face and body. He also suffered a severe blow to the right side of the skull post-acid attack. We think it's when he tried to leave the car. It also appears that at some point he wasn't alone inside."

"I take it the acid has delayed things?"

"Always has to be made safe, you want to see the clothing they're having to wear. Pritchett looks like Neil bloody Armstrong!"

"Has he been identified?"

The CSM nodded. "He's Abdul Kumar, forty-three. That's from the documents and the car's registration. Married, five children. He doesn't have much face, which makes formal ID difficult until he's back on the table and DNA is taken. According to his wife, he was supposed to be visiting a business acquaintance in Blackburn. He told her that he would be late back."

"Whose case?"

The CSM smiled at Cyril.

***

Owen was at his desk when Cyril walked in.

"Five minutes, my office with a brew, please, Owen."

After hanging up his coat he sat at his desk and put his face into the open palm of his hand and massaged his temple with his thumb and fingers. It was going to be a long day. Owen walked in carrying the cup and saucer and a plate of custard creams.

"I can see from your expression, sir, that you need an intake of calories. I'll just pop and get my brew."

Within minutes Owen was back. One custard cream remained on the plate.

"So, what did you discover from your Northumberland trip?" Cyril enquired concentrating on sipping his tea. Owen was correct, the biscuits had immediately given him a boost.

"It was the boyfriend, the body in the hole. We've discovered the missing Ben. Not a dog after all. I can only make the scenario up but Mr Edge got his daughter pregnant, boyfriend went to sort it out but failed. Killed by a blow to the head. We'll never know if it were deliberate or accidental. Body cut and put in a secure area and then covered by a false wall in either the attic or the bedroom."

"Case closed?" Cyril finished the last of his tea. "What of the red toe nails?"

"This is how I know that she, Emma, is telling the truth. She mentioned the last time she saw Ben. They'd paddled in the river and then she painted her nails and for a laugh, she painted his. She told me they both lay there on the riverbank waggling their toes waiting for them to dry. Ruth felt from her responses that she truly loved him. When she spoke of these moments there was gentleness, sincerity and in some way a real sadness in her voice that she never conveyed when speaking about any other part of her early life. Funny thing, she never broke down at all at that point. She gave the impression that everything was in the past and therefore best forgotten. The two people who gave her the most grief in her life were dead and so was the one who had offered a glimpse of true happiness. Her words, sir."

"So where did she think he went?"

"Ruth asked that too." Owen pointed to the remaining custard cream.

Cyril offered the plate.

"There was a letter waiting for her the next day saying that he had had to go away for a while but he'd find her wherever she might be. She showed us the letter. She was a bit weepy then so I left Ruth to do her magic. He obviously wrote it before he went to see her father."

Cyril raised his hand to his inside jacket pocket and felt the sharp edge of the envelope. There was a pause. "Or the father wrote it knowing what he'd just done."

Owen noticed Cyril's expression as he moved his hand away from the inside of his jacket. "Are you all right, sir?"

Cyril nodded. "Well done. Will Ruth be liaising? We'll close the case down providing, that is, that no further evidence comes to light."

"She'll report as and when. What about you, sir? What about the crosses and the hair? "

Cyril recovered his composure. "Theological confusion, Owen. Blinded by chapter and bloody verse. I've left it with DC Richmond to look into. However, we have a body found this morning in a layby on Brimham Rocks Road, acid attack and then, we believe, a blow to the head. Asian male and as a bonus I appear to be SIO. I don't know about meeting a vicar today, I must have killed a priest in my last life."

Owen smiled and popped the whole custard cream into his mouth. "If you want a job doing, give it to a busy man one of my old bosses used to always say."

Cyril watched flecks of masticated biscuit escape from his moving lips. He sighed and thought of his hand wrapped around the throat of some ancient cleric.

***

Cyril wandered around Julie's office. He valued time alone there, time he could spend inspecting the collection of specimens for a few private moments, a veritable treasure trove of anatomical objects placed on shelves, stored in jars. The pickled penis always distracted him and he tried not to look too closely. What did attract him was one jar sitting on her desk. He had not seen it before. He picked up the jar and turned it in his hands, like a child admiring a fish in a jam jar. Julie entered.

"Typical detective! You can leave nothing alone." She kissed his cheek. "It's a human tongue."

Cyril turned the jar through three hundred and sixty degrees before announcing assuredly, "Strongest muscle in the human body."

"Wrong, Mr Holmes."

"It's a well-known fact!" Cyril protested.

"Sorry, Cyril, actually that's not true. What's true, the tongue never suffers from fatigue, it's not one muscle but made up of eight... muscular hydrostats... an elephant's trunk or an octopus's tentacles are made the same way."

Cyril put the jar back on the desk. He found himself moving his tongue around his mouth.

"You see we can use our tongue in many ways, curl it forward, back and sideways, stretch and retract." Julie demonstrated. "It's a vital organ of articulation, taste and sense."

"What have you been able to discover about Mr Kumar?"

"He wasn't on the moor taking the air. That was some mess and owing to the acid used it took some neutralising. Let me tell you what we have for starters but we need to look further now the corpse is back here. The body has suffered extensive burns to the face, hands, genitals and legs. Very strong acid was used. Firstly, and this is only a guess at this stage, concentrated nitric acid to the face and upper torso. This would have blinded him and caused severe pain. Then it appears that a concentrated form of hydrofluoric acid was poured over the genital area. You can see from the photographs how the body has reacted, the flesh has turned from normal flesh tint to white in places. The skin is peeling, this is where the hydrofluoric acid has attacked. The colour has been drained from the flesh as it penetrates the layers and enters the bone, a direct result of myoglobin being destroyed. What the acid does when entering the body is to replace all of the calcium-containing compounds. The most important of these tells your heart to keep beating and when that is destroyed... there is no treatment, no cure. You can only die."

Cyril looked at the images on her computer screen, his glasses perched on the end of his nose. "So what quantity does it take to do that?"

Julie turned the screen back round. "If you were to put your index finger into this acid you would have some discomfort but it's all that would be needed to kill you. HF eats through glass, Cyril. A dermal exposure of seventy per cent concentration HF to two point five per cent of your body area will result in death."

"How's it transported?" Cyril sat up and stared at his index finger.

"PTFE bottles, the stuff that lines your frying pan, it's an inert material. However, HF is made from hydrogen fluoride gas. The emergency services had to ensure it was safe to enter the site and they've their standard operating procedures for chemical contamination. What's interesting is the fact that there was evidence of the rear nearside door being used more than the other; significantly, the rear window was also smashed. I've a theory that whoever did this broke the window to allow any build up of gas to escape and therefore safeguard any innocent who stumbled on the site."

"A caring, vicious murderer, helpful! How's the guy who found him, Mr Wells wasn't it?"

"Sensibly, he moved away after looking at the victim. As you've seen he's not pretty. Wells kept his distance and called the police. He was taken away in severe shock. The body and the vehicle have been cleaned to neutralise the HF. Severe drenching with water so don't hold your breath for much forensic evidence. The vehicle will be taken for a thorough forensic investigation but.... We have the body here. It's isolated and will need special handling. Will you be attending or will you send Owen?"

"What about the blow to the head?"

"Superficial on inspection, probably self inflicted whilst thrashing about in the back seat."

"If this acid, this HF is so deadly how did the murderer get their hands on the stuff. Surely you'll not be able to buy it at B&Q?"

"It's used in industry, glass etching, electronics but a good high school chemistry teacher could produce enough in a morning by making HF gas using calcium fluoride and sulphuric acid and then progressing from there. You'd need a fume cupboard..." Aware that she had gone a little too technical, she smiled.

"Owen will be attending."

Chapter Fourteen

Cyril stood outside Harrogate Police Station looking through the trees and then across the fields to the far horizon. He inhaled the menthol vapour and felt his shoulders relax. Ruth, the Family Liaison Officer, had parked and was just coming into the building when she saw Cyril.

"Taking the air, sir?"

He turned and smiled. "Happiest place to live in the United Kingdom, Ruth."

"Where?"

"Harrogate. It won that accolade a while back. Might still be in the running. You wouldn't believe that from where I'm standing, you wouldn't think we'd be so busy would you if that were the case?" He turned and winked at her. "Been to visit the family?"

She smiled. "Happiest place, really? I must just meet all the unhappy ones and Mrs Kumar is no exception. Beautiful home, it's a new build, affluent area, Dalesway, I think is its official title, just off the A59 and rather nice too. It was obvious that a number of people had arrived, probably extended family, to support Mr Kumar's wife and children."

"Busy week, Ruth!" Cyril turned and smiled at the FLO who simply nodded. "Are you fine with this case coming so close to the last?"

"No problem, I'm on leave in two days. I'll keep the Northumberland case. I was surprised when Owen mentioned that the Edges's son had been a heavy drug user and that, according to the post mortem, this was a contributing factor in the motorcycle accident. No other vehicle involved, no witnesses. Found nearly twenty-four hours after his death. He crashed on a bend owing to excessive speed, ended up in

76

woodland concealed from the road. That information and the drugs had been kept from Emma. She's got a new life and emotionally is very strong. *Hard as nails* according to Owen!"

A cloud of vapour erupted from Cyril's right nostril. "This one, however, needs a little more specialist support. Always a sensitive one considering the awkward and somewhat compromising situation in which her husband's body was found."

"I called and saw Mrs Kumar with the support from a Muslim FSO who's now been assigned. Fortunately, she's not known personally within this local, Muslim community. It will help if there are any psychological or religious barriers. Risk assessments have been completed and I'll liaise, if necessary on my return but she'll be attending briefings and debriefs. By the way, she said in passing that you've met before, Mada Amber. Ring any bells?"

Cyril felt himself blush a little as he put a face to the name. It didn't go unnoticed as Ruth continued speaking.

"There's no objection to autopsy on religious grounds and she fully understands that a release date for the body cannot be confirmed yet."

"Good, good." He quickly turned away to look at the view. "We've managed to collect his IT equipment, it's with the tech people to see if there's anything that may help, also the equipment from his place of work. Presently we're contacting the associate her husband was allegedly meeting. I take it Mada knows what she's looking for?"

Ruth turned. "Of course. She'll collect and collate the sensitive ante-mortem data. Must get on." Ruth walked towards the main entrance. She stopped and turned back. "Mada said that it was a long time ago!"

Cyril turned. "A lot of water's passed beneath the bridge let's say, Ruth. An awful lot!"

In his mind Cyril was back in Chester. He remembered rowing on the River Dee. Mada was smiling, sitting at the back of the boat giving directions and laughing whilst trailing her hand

77

in the water. She'd occasionally flick the water and then giggle. They were both younger. As he had said a lot of water had gone under Chester chain bridge since then. He smiled at the memory.

***

Owen stood looking at the corpse. Julie was dressed in a complete protective suit. The body was on a downdraft stainless steel bench allowing any contaminants to be sucked away.

"It's a little different today, Owen. If it gets upsetting try the standing on your toes trick and if that fails, just leave."

He waved and stood on his toes, remembering what she had told him on a previous occasion.

"Abdul Kumar. Asian male, forty-three years old. As you see, extensive facial damage including eyes and mouth. What is interesting is the severe and intense damage that we see concentrated to the groin and lower limb area; it would suggest that this section was targeted with a larger acid concentration. Targeting the head and face was a deliberate ploy to cause the maximum shock while suffering maximum trauma. The penis, you might not be able to distinguish, has melted and blended with the other severely damaged tissue on the thighs, particularly the right and the lower abdomen, here. However, if you look at the screen you can see the close-up view from my head camera."

Owen looked at the large screen opposite and waved. Wherever Julie looked, Owen received close up images.

"Here and here we see the remnants of the ring of a condom." Julie identified the areas using a pointer. "There will be other traces of the condom blended within the flesh. The fact that he was wearing a condom will aid your investigation." She turned her heavily protected face towards Owen. He saw himself now on the screen opposite. "Someone may well have been in the car prior to the attack. That person may have been the attacker and that person could've been male or female. At this stage we cannot say for certain."

"Why use two different acids?" Owen asked.

"Good question. One, the nitric acid was used first to stun and blind, causing immediate shock, pain and panic, and the other to kill. The person would've survived the attack by nitric acid. They'd have suffered life-changing injuries but they would have lived. The use of hydrofluoric acid gave them no chance. It was murder and we can't rule out that it's most likely a revenge attack. Vitriolage, as it is known, is a common form of attack in Bangladesh and Pakistan. If you check, you'll see that cases are on the rise. However, it's spreading to all parts of the world but it's most common in South Asia. It's meant to torture, maim and disfigure. Death is not the reason for doing it, simply revenge to make the recipient of the attack suffer. In Asian countries it tends to be related to relationships and sex. From the statistics I checked this morning, these attacks are on the rise for many different reasons."

"Surely transporting it and using it put the attacker in danger also?"

"Not if they were waiting, prepared and secure in the knowledge that they'd taken all the necessary precautions. This attack wasn't random, Owen, it was planned."

"So a third party? Involved with the person who was with the victim in the car if it were a planned attack?"

"Slow down, Owen. Evidence, evidence and then more evidence is needed. We can't assume anything at this stage."

"Can we assume he was there for sex?"

"I think we can safely say that that was the case. However, we are only just beginning. Anything from Forensics on the car or the site?"

"Cyril's department." Owen smiled.

Chapter Fifteen

Cyril and Owen sat in The Coach and Horses each trying to work out the Tour de Yorkshire anagram that was cleverly printed on the top of the table.

"A puzzle! A bit like the numbers written on the crosses, Owen. They're there for a reason. Each number must have a relevance, if not why bother?"

"Bloody hate the things." Owen muttered as he swiftly drank half the pint leaving him with a froth moustache. His sleeve came in handy yet again. "Bloody crap at these sorts of things. My mate was mustard at them when I was in Vice in Bradford. Had a book full. He'd spend all his break solving them."

"What, anagrams or number puzzles?" Cyril sipped his beer and took a pen and notebook to write down and rearrange the given letters. "Jervaulx Abbey!" he said triumphantly.

"Well done!" There was little enthusiasm in Owen's tone. "He did both. I remember he used to lick his pencil before he started a new puzzle, kind of a ritual. Seemed to have the desired effect."

Cyril looked at Owen and frowned. "Really. April has her own theories but…" He felt his phone vibrate in his pocket. He read the text and looked carefully at the accompanying image. It showed a thin, scarlet thread, tied to what was described as the rear-view mirror of Kumar's Volvo. It dangled next to a car air freshener. Cyril slid the phone across the table.

"Just through from Forensics. According to the scientists it's not the string from another freshener, it's a very different material. Read it."

Owen put the glass down and collected the phone. He read through the report sliding his finger on the screen. He then looked at Cyril.

"Plaited human hair?" Owen looked up with a puzzled expression drawn on his face. "Scarlet human hair? What the… disgusting that is if you ask me!"

Cyril slowly recited something April had said. "Though your sins be as scarlet, they shall be as white as snow; though they be… I can't recall the rest."

"From the meeting with the vicar?" Owen asked handing the phone back.

Cyril nodded. "Gideon. He left him a single page of the Bible on which that was written; it was wrapped and tied with a scarlet thread. Deliberately handed it to Reverend Ian Fella, the vicar, the night Gideon disappeared." He looked at the image on the phone and drummed the table with his fingers. "Coincidentally, we now find crosses linked to sealed packets of dyed hair spread around in various and varied locations."

Owen finished his pint. "Another? It'll help you think."

"No, work. Now!"

Cyril quickly made four calls.

***

Shakti, Stuart Park, April Richmond and Mada Amber were waiting when Cyril and Owen came into the briefing room.

"Sorry to interrupt your evening but we have a strong link connecting Gideon, our missing saint, and the newly found crosses and hair. I imagine that he's no longer missing. If he is, someone is cleverly using the connection, as far-fetched as that might seem. Let's recap." Cyril stood and moved to an empty whiteboard, collecting a pen on the way. "We find a cross, a Christian symbol attached by a line to a packet of hair, a collection of hair comprising different DNA. It's been dyed scarlet. Can we assume that's another symbolic gesture?" He looked at each member of the team and saw three nod in agreement. April remained motionless but deep in thought. "We also believe that the hair has been taken at random. As we've had no one complain that someone's been taking cuttings from passers-by on the streets, we can make a safe and educated guess that it's been collected from the bin of one or more hairdressers. In the packets we then discover two DNA matches. One, a familial link to Gideon Fletcher and secondly a direct DNA link to Tracy Phillips who, like Gideon, simply vanished. Now, for whatever reason we find the packets of hair, a newspaper is discovered in which this message is found and, like the crosses, we believe the paper to have been left deliberately. We now have a body, that of Abdul Kumar." Cyril drew a large question mark on the board. "Thoughts, please."

Owen was the first to speak. "Am I right in thinking that the two matched DNA samples were found in the same packet?"

"Good man, I think you're right. Please check."

Owen went to the nearest computer to draw up the relevant file.

There was a moment's silence until Shakti spoke. "You haven't mentioned the link that's been found to make Kumar relevant to the two cases, sir."

The others looked at Shakti, Cyril and then Owen who was still busy on the computer.

"Hair, for what we know, human hair. It was hanging from the rear-view mirror of Kumar's car; a thin thread of plaited human hair. Here's your starter for ten everyone. Colour?" Cyril looked at each officer in turn and concentrated on their lips as he saw them each mouth, *scarlet.*

Cyril smiled at his team.

"*Like Rahab, all Christians have a scarlet cord hanging in the window of their soul.* Those were the final words that Gideon said to the vicar, sir, if you recall. He followed it up by saying- " April announced before Cyril cut in.

"*Even you.* Were his final parting words if my memory serves me correctly, April."

April smiled. "Correct, it's here in my report."

"They say the windows of your soul are your eyes," Stuart added.

"I believe that they were the first part of Kumar that was attacked, his eyes. Nitric acid destroyed his eyelids and his eyes."

"Kumar's Muslim and not Christian," April pointed out.

"DNA of the hair?" Shakti asked.

"As soon as, as soon as."

Cyril turned to the board. "So let's just consider that for some reason Gideon is back with us more than likely in a different guise. We know that before he had his Damascus moment, he was an utter bastard. He demonstrated little tolerance of other people's race or religion. Now we have a link to him and we find that we have a racist attack."

Owen glanced at his watch. "First thing tomorrow, Stuart, a list of all the Fletchers within a fifty mile radius. We know his age and his height so you should be able to whittle that down."

"Bit of a long shot. Surely he'll have changed his name if he's back for trouble."

"If we don't check, then we'll never know. April, get an appointment with the vicar tomorrow as soon as. Ring now. See if he can tell you what Gideon meant by his final words. He might have a skeleton in his cupboard. He might talk to you."

Cyril caught Owen's sudden head movement. "Owen?"

"It's just your saying skeleton in the cupboard made me think of Boffey."

Cyril looked at him. "There's no connection with this. All that was closed down, questions answered, yes?"

"Yes, I'm sure. It was just the thought." Owen looked down and rubbed his chin.

Cyril wiped the board clean.

Owen and Stuart Park left the room leaving only Mada and April.

"Sir."

Cyril turned and smiled.

"You know about the true Gideon?" April asked looking at Mada and then Cyril.

"What about him?"

"Gideon was a man who was willing to do exactly what God wanted him to do regardless of his own judgement or plans. Could our Gideon live now both lives as one? I'm trying to get my head round it myself. You witnessed a complete change after he served his prison sentence. What if his characters are in some kind of conflict, one is controlling the other regardless of the consequences?"

"I don't have answers to those sort of questions, April. I can see what you mean but whether someone with split personalities can find one of their characters controlling the other… like the good voice and the bad… psychopathic? I don't know."

Mada said nothing.

"Let's see what tomorrow brings and what results are found from the forensics on the car. Hopefully, Mada, you'll have more on Kumar's background soon. Now let's call it a day."

As they left Owen caught April's arm. "Can you spare me a couple of minutes?"

April smiled. "Sure."

"The list from the Bible, St Mark, I think you said, the list of human weaknesses."

"Yes, do you think I'm wrong?"

"No, it's not that. I understand some but not others. What's the difference between adulteries and fornication? What's lasciviousness? As for an evil eye?"

April smiled. "I'll have a list for you tomorrow and chat through it."

Owen smiled. "Thanks. Don't want to appear thick! Never been one for church stuff."

Chapter Sixteen

Cyril walked home, his collar pulled up, protection against the chill breeze. As he crossed The Stray, he could see the lights of The Coach and Horses clearly visible, a siren's call. *Not tonight Bennett,* he said to himself. He had an appointment with the past that somehow he knew was going to encroach into the present.

***

Cyril needed space. If it were possible, he would have created a vacuum, devoid of the past and the future, isolated from human guilt, acrimony, resentment and bitterness but he knew that to be impossible as he could feel his hopefulness bubble up within him like methane from the depth of an ancient mire ready to break the placid, dark surface. He wondered how the contents of the letter might disturb his life as he fondled the creased envelope. He smelled it again allowing what he believed to be a recognised aroma to linger a moment longer.

He moved over to the table lamp and read his name again, Mr C V Bennett. The blue, elegant handwriting was the only clue he needed to realise the sender's identity. The small-bladed letter opener slid through the top neatly but with a degree of reluctance as if he were about to release the genie from within. He held it away slightly. Nothing appeared. He withdrew the letter allowing the envelope to fall onto the table. Opening the folded paper he read:

My dearest Cyril…

***

April could not call it a day. The idea of what she had been trying to convey swam in her mind in a desperate attempt to make some sort of sense; like a toothache it nagged. She looked at the illuminated hands on the bedside clock that cast a faint, blue glow. She just could not stop her mind from racing. She got up and went to make a cup of hot milk hoping that would work soporific miracles and would be able to make her sleep; it was not to be.

She sipped the milk and moved to the computer before reluctantly lifting the lid of what she knew would be an electronic can of worms. Once the light from the screen struck her eyes she was fully awake. She typed *dissociative-identity-disorder* into the search engine but within ten minutes of researching she knew it was not the answer for which she was looking.

"Could somebody have more than one personality and one of those personalities bully and coerce the other or others?" she said out loud knowing full well that no answer would follow. She recalled reading about a mental illness in some supplement magazine and she struggled to remember the medical term. She sat back sipping the hot milk and then from her tired and confused mind it came to her. She typed in the words *socialised and integrated psychopath.*

***

The light had only just cracked the dark eastern sky bringing an unnatural turquoise hue. Some streetlights were still on, each with a glowing, surrounding nimbus, reluctant to accept the day's advent. The garage door slowly climbed and rolled upwards with a degree of morning lethargy, the sounds seeming to add an appropriate accompaniment as the insipid new light began to flood the garage floor. Graham Baker started the car, selected drive and moved out of the garage. A quick press of the remote key brought the door down behind him. He checked his watch.

***

April Richmond had woken with a start, her head positioned almost on the laptop keyboard. She lifted her head cautiously noticing the half drunk mug of now cold milk to her left, the surface, a wrinkled magnolia skin. As she moved she disturbed the computer and the screen suddenly lit, stabbing her eyes and revealing the last of her nocturnal searches. She stretched trying to force some kind of movement back into her cramped torso whilst focussing on the screen. It was the time in the top right-hand corner that generated a more positive acceptance of the morning.

"Bloody hell!" There was nobody to hear her. She had ninety minutes to make her appointment with the vicar.

***

Crescent Gardens was devoid of pedestrians at this time of the morning but had anyone been walking past they would have failed to identify Angie Rhodes sitting, knees tucked towards her chest and the hood of her jacket pulled covering most of her face. She stared out from the back corner of the glass-roofed shelter across the gardens towards the Kursaal, the Royal Hall, a magnificent building that was attached to the Conference Centre. The beauty of the building and the gardens were wasted on her. All she worried about was the money, one of the two packets, now safely stashed, and the next fag.

She had arrived at the location at the specified time and had been rewarded to find what she had been anticipating. She fondled the folded twenty-pound note held in her pocket and smiled before rolling a cigarette. The newspaper, in which she had found the packets and the money, was now under her backside, an insulating layer between her and the cold Yorkshire flagstones. She spat a small piece of tobacco from her lips and then inhaled. A wisp of smoke curled and vanished as quickly as her smile. She drew on the cigarette once more before flicking the stub away.

She stood, placed the padded envelope marked with a cross on the ledge behind her as instructed, thrust her hands into her pockets and left the shelter before turning up towards the Royal Pump Room Museum. She neither noticed the parked car amongst many nor did she notice the driver slumped behind the wheel, as she turned left up the cobbled road. He on the other hand observed her carefully and waited a few moments before leaving the car.

Within thirty minutes another hand reached for the same shelf but collected a different envelope. The transaction had come full circle.

Chapter Seventeen

April walked to the front door of a modern bungalow situated a short walk from the church. The original vicarage had long since been sold. Its stables, coach house and three-quarters of an acre seemed excessive accommodation in today's secular society. However, she was sure that the vicar found this property far more manageable. She checked her watch; she was a little early. Considering the traffic she had made good progress. There had been only one short delay when she found herself stuck behind a large farm Leviathan masquerading as a modern-day tractor, the only down side to the journey.

Ringing the bell she waited but there was no response. She tried again, but nothing. She checked her watch for the second time and then her diary *Clipton Vicarage, 08.30.* She moved towards one of the windows and looked in. All was dark. *Maybe he's delayed at the church,* she thought and walked down the path. The church was also quiet. A lady looked across at her whilst cutting the tufted grass between the gravestones with a scythe.

"May I help you?" She stopped and stood resting on the curved, wooden handle.

April paused, slightly startled, but then raised a hand in greeting whilst having immediate thoughts of the Grim Reaper. It was the gravestones that did it. "I'm looking for Reverend Fella. I had an appointment with him at the vicarage this morning but he didn't answer so I wondered if he'd been delayed in the church."

"What's today?"

"Tuesday."

"He takes a service in the next village today. Probably running late. One can never make plans."

89

April looked at the scythe.

"The first real cut of the year. We're an ecological church, trying to encourage bio-diversity within the church grounds rather than just the dead." The woman laughed at her own joke. "Good way of keeping fit too. We haven't managed to encourage any Ross Poldarks yet but we're ever optimistic." They both laughed at that. "If I see him I'll tell him. Whom shall I say called?"

"DC April Richmond."

"Police? I'll let him know." With that she moved to find another short clump of grass to swing at.

"Good luck with Poldark!" April shouted unsure as to why she had said it. She knew that the news of the police making enquiries would travel fast; village gossip was a wonderful system of communicating other people's business.

April dialled the number of the vicarage and his mobile but both went to answerphone. She would try once more at the vicarage and then go.

***

Graham Baker pressed the button on the internal garage wall and watched as the door slowly closed. He glanced at the newspaper headline and read briefly about the murder on the moor before tucking the paper under his arm and moving down the corridor, a stick in either hand. He tossed the paper onto his chair in the lounge, rested his two sticks against the arm before turning the handle and opening the first door on the opposite side of the hallway. The curtains were still drawn and the room was washed in relative darkness. There was no movement only the sound of somebody sleeping; the breath was rhythmic and shallow. Opening the door a little wider allowed the light to steal further into the room. He smiled before walking to the bedside cabinet to retrieve the cup, checking to see if the contents had been drained. They had. She would sleep a while longer, he thought as he looked at the illuminated clock before moving out and quietly closing the door.

***

Cyril had enjoyed his walk to work as usual; he treated it as quality thinking time. He had collected his paper and a couple of bottles of liquid for his electronic cigarette. The sky gave a clue as to the day's weather and he felt a little more optimistic. The days were lengthening, making the morning commute more enjoyable, but today his mind flicked back to the contents of the letter and somehow his world seemed momentarily a little darker. In his heart he knew he should have left the letter unopened.

Owen was already at his desk. He had printed off an email from April Richmond. She had answered his questions with more clarity. He read and smiled. Cyril checked his watch and shook it before glancing at the clock on the wall.

"Morning, Owen. Early?" Cyril slipped off his coat.

"Couldn't sleep." Owen folded the sheet and tucked it into his pocket. "This case is really puzzling me. For some reason I keep thinking of Boffey… I know. I know." He held up both hands as if to stop Cyril from giving his anticipated response. "There's no logic to my reasoning, the case is virtually closed but something inside keeps nagging. With your permission I just want to keep it on the shelf until all this is over."

"Don't ignore the gut, Owen. Forensics on the car?"

"I'll see you in the Incident Room. There's something else come through too."

Smirthwaite, Shakti and Park were already there. Cyril greeted them as he entered. "Morning everyone. What news from the scientists?" He rubbed his hands together as if looking forward to what lay ahead.

Stuart Park was the one controlling the screen's remote. The blue police badge image quickly changed and the photographs appeared of the plaited hair. "It's human, it's dyed scarlet, approximately twelve centimetres in length. Bound at the top with strong adhesive, which also glued a length of silk ribbon to the hair; that's how it was secured to the mirror. The bottom of the plait has been secured by looped cotton; it's a standard three-strand plait. According to Mada, the family know nothing of the plaited hair attached to the Volvo's mirror. It certainly wasn't there that afternoon when Mrs Kumar used the vehicle to go shopping. There was only the air freshener, so can we assume this was placed there on the evening of the attack?"

"I don't think so at this stage. I know it's on the mirror but some drivers don't use it. If you're not looking for it and particularly as there was already something hanging from it, I don't believe we can," Cyril stated adamantly.

Stuart accepted it. "Now for the interesting bit. We have more than one DNA match from the plait." He paused allowing the information to sink in. "We have a familial link to Gideon, a link to Tracy Phillips. We had those before but this time we have a bonus, we have one more. We took Mrs Kumar's DNA as a routine procedure for elimination purposes but there are strands of hair within the plait that match her DNA."

Cyril placed his elbows on the table, linking his hands before resting his chin on the back of his fingers. He stared at the image. The pause was palpable.

"That's not all." Stuart Park brought another picture to the screen. "This is the rear door. Where the vehicle was positioned in the layby there is only one real feature and that's this tree. Here you see the proximity, the only place anyone could remain concealed would be here. However, remember it was dark and the occupant of the car was busy. Consequently, the attacker could have come from any direction. As you can see, this layby has a covering of loose tarmac and gravel." He flicked another image to the screen. It showed small stones on the car's floor. "Although the car was decontaminated, they still found gravel in both rear foot wells that matched the area. It can be safely assumed that at some stage two people occupied the rear seats. We can deduce that both driver and passenger moved from the front seats to the rear. We've also found a number of DNA traces that have yet to be identified. These will be from previous passengers. Because of the cleansing after the acid attack there are fewer than we'd normally expect."

"Link with Mada and find out where Kumar's wife has her hair cut. Does she go out or does someone come to the house? Do we have a percentage content?" Cyril asked.

Stuart looked at his notes. "A few strands only of each identifiable source."

Shakti was the next to speak. She slid some files across the table. "The tech boys have been busy on Kumar's computers. Those at the house and business were clean. However, we found a computer in the garage. We were informed it was broken and never used. To the inexperienced it certainly gave that impression. It wasn't. If you look in the file you can see some of the images taken from it."

Owen slid the four images from the file and spread them in front of himself and Cyril. Each showed a naked female. Each image was explicit and on none was the face visible.

"There are movies too."

"Kumar?" Cyril asked.

"We believe so. Sir, we've also been working with our Lancashire colleagues. The businessman cited as being visited on the evening knew nothing of the meeting. He has given a statement that he rarely sees Kumar, most of the business is done either over the phone or on the Internet. On the night in question he was having a meal with his mother in Blackburn and has the receipt. He's been fully co-operative."

"I take it we've checked his computers and his communications with Kumar?" Cyril asked whilst pushing the images back into the folder. He could detect Shakti's discomfort. He knew her feelings about the previous grooming cases in Newcastle and Rochdale, and tried to offer her some support. He smiled at her. "Are you okay with this, Shak?"

Even though she understood his concern she looked him in the eye. "It's my job, sir. Thanks for your consideration."

She returned the smile. "It's in hand now that there's a link between the two, albeit a tenuous one. The previous errors made with regards to other similar cases have brought a renewed focus to police investigation. No more fear of upsetting minority groups, I for one am pleased to say. We are also investigating all of Kumar's contacts."

Cyril nodded to her. "Well done!"

Chapter Eighteen

April approached the vicarage. She stood and wrote a note to pop through the letterbox. She pressed the bell and waited. Nothing. She opened the flap on the door to push the folded paper through but the door opened. The unexpected movement startled her.

"Hello!" She called pushing the door a little wider. "Reverend Fella, are you there?" She looked down the path feeling a little uncertain as to what to do before opening the door fully. She called again but received no response. Moving cautiously into the small hallway, she noticed a newspaper lying on the mat. Calling out again, she slipped on a pair of nitrile gloves. She looked in each room but they were all empty. She went into the bathroom and checked the shower tray. It was dry. She had ventured only into the rooms where the doors were left ajar, the others were closed. Knocking on each one she called the Reverend's name before entering. Still nothing but she observed that all the beds had been made. Once in the kitchen, she touched the kettle, it was cold. She felt anxious. She placed the note on the kitchen table and left closing the front door.

She decided to call on the closest neighbour so walked up the path. The front door opened before she had reached half way. Showing her warrant card, she introduced herself.

"DC Richmond. I've just been to the vicarage but it appears that nobody's at home even though I had an appointment with Reverend Fella at eight-thirty this morning. The front door's open too. Is that normal?"

The young man smiled. "Nothing unusual, bit absent-minded is Ian, thinks Clipton is still in the 1930s, not that he's old enough to even remember the 50s. I keep telling him he's too trusting. I'll keep an eye open for him, neighbourhood watch and all that." The man smiled as if that was the end of the conversation.

"Have you seen him today?" April asked determined to find someone who knew of his whereabouts that morning.

"Come to think of it no. He's usually in the next village today for the morning service. Maybe he's been delayed. Some of his elderly parishioners can talk for Yorkshire. If I see him, I'll tell him you called…" He waited as if for April to remind him of her name.

"Detective Constable Richmond."

She left and walked back to the vicarage. The neighbour watched, the flickering curtain, the obvious giveaway. She rang his house number again and heard it ring out and then go to answerphone. She then dialled his mobile number. To her surprise, that too rang out, this time in a different location in the house. She hung up. She had a strange feeling about this. She contacted Owen.

***

Cyril stood looking at the whiteboards around the Incident Room. Evidence from the three cases was now being cross-referenced. He looked at the images of Gideon. "What are you up to, Gideon Fletcher?" he whispered to himself.

Owen's phone vibrated and shimmied across the table.

"Owen." He listened. "Give me a minute." Owen turned to Cyril.

"The vicar didn't show for the appointment this morning. There's no one in the house and the door was open. His mobile's in the house." Owen handed the phone to Cyril.

"Go to the church where he held the service this morning, see if you can find anyone who saw him leave. Then return to the vicarage. Call me again when you're back."

***

Within ten minutes she had parked in front of the small church. She tried the sturdy, wooden door but it was locked. She walked around the flagged yard; there was nobody about, the village seemed empty. She looked at the bench and read the tarnished, engraved brass plaque.

Donated by the Scouts and Guides in memory of Princess Diana

April stared at it, amazed how the time had flown since her tragic death. Somehow she could recall where she had been when she heard the news. A car passed and brought her back to the present. Looking across the road to the shop, she decided that a visit there would be the best place to start her enquiries. She entered to the cheery ringing of a bell and then was greeted with a smile.

"I'm looking for the vicar who should have been at the church this morning." She pointed unnecessarily to the church. "Have you seen him today?"

"No, this morning's Eucharist was cancelled. Ian, the vicar, rang to say he wasn't too well. Is something wrong, love?"

April bluffed her way out of the shop assuring the shopkeeper that all was well but she was followed to the door.

"Usually comes on his bicycle, lovely man. Keeps the community here going. First time in many years that I've known him suffer any illness. Never misses."

"Who took his call?"

"Mrs Fleet, she looks after the church. Married, husband drives wagons on the continent, never here see, and therefore she has time on her hands. I've offered her my husband when hers is away so that I can have time but she refuses. You wouldn't want him for a weekend or two would you love?" She laughed out loud. She moved a little closer, "Mind, some say the vicar pops in rather a lot!" She winked and touched the side of her nose.

97

"Where can I find her?" April was feeling the lack of sleep and her patience was fast draining away.

"Next to the church. If you're going, take her paper for me, love."

April crossed the road and immediately noticed the sign hanging on the front door of Fleet's house. *I'm in the garden*. She walked to the side of the end-terraced house and turned down between the gable and the wall that separated the house from the churchyard. The breeze suddenly stiffened as it was channelled within the narrow gap. She then noticed Mrs Fleet, she was busy feeding some bantams that flocked and fussed affectionately around her feet. Deep in conversation, she was calling each by name, oblivious that someone was watching.

"Mrs Fleet!" April called whilst waving the newspaper.

She turned briefly and lifted the bucket a little higher as if in a wave. "A minute, just giving my girls their breakfast." She smiled unperturbed by the intrusion of a total stranger. "Just stand still and Ralph'll leave you be."

It was only then did April notice the very large dog that was sprawled next to the kennel, his eyes clearly focussed on her. She decided to do just that, stand still.

Mrs Fleet emptied the remaining contents of the bucket, dropped a few Brussels sprout stems around the run and made her way towards April. Her wellington boots appeared two sizes too large. "Can I help you?"

"I was asked to drop in your paper. I'm looking for Reverend Fella and called in at the shop. I was directed to you."

"Of all the days you come looking for him." She shook her head and walked across to stroke the dog's ears. "Murphy's Law I think they call it. He's ill. Rang me this morning. Sounded proper rough too, didn't know it were him. First time in a lot of years that he's called in sick. I can give you his address if you like." She took the newspaper and tucked it into her wellington boot. "Few more little jobs to do before I can read that and then Ralph needs his…" she whispered… "walk."

The dog stood, his legs appearing too long for the size of his body. Now suddenly alert, he shook himself. "Too clever by half this dog! Anything else?"

"What was the matter?"

"Didn't say, seemed a little rushed but I guess it was a throat infection or the like, sounded hoarse, raspy. I told him to take good care and he hung up. Probably that man flu!" She chuckled to herself and then looked skyward as if expecting some kind of divine retribution to break from the blue.

"Did he ring from his house line or his mobile?"

Mrs Fleet stood and stared at April. Her facial expression said everything but the words quickly followed in case there was any doubt. "He rang. How do I know what phone he used?"

"Was his the last call you received today, you see I'm from the police and that's a vital piece of information. If it were the last call you received then by dialling 1471, I can see the number he called you on." April showed her ID. She could now see the anxiety appear on Mrs Fleet's face.

"He is all right?"

"Yes, I just need to check that number."

"The house phone, it's there on the kitchen wall. He is all right, isn't he?"

As April entered, Mrs Fleet unhooked the chain that fastened the dog to the kennel and she attached a lead to his collar, moving him toward the bantams and the fence. The dog put his nose to the wire and watched them scratch and peck. April left the house and waved her thanks, eager to return to the vicarage. She was not expecting a *no number stored* message. She saw Mrs Fleet turn to come towards her whilst tugging at the lead and grumbling at Ralph. April took the opportunity to slip down the passageway to her car.

***

Cyril answered her call.

"Uncomfortable feeling about this, sir." She described her morning whilst driving back.

"When you get to the vicarage, wait outside, stay with your car, I'm going to get one of the locals to do the search with you. Everything! Garage, shed, garden, loft the lot. Touch as little as possible."

Cyril moved to one of the seated officers and jotted down Fella's details. "Get as much info on him as possible, please make it a priority." He rested a hand on his shoulder. "As soon as." He smiled and went to his room.

***

The officer brought some overshoes and gloves. "I was told we should use these, just in case. It could be nothing and then again…" His sentence trailed away and he bent to put on the overshoes.

As before, the bungalow was empty, nothing appeared to have been disturbed. The adjoining garage was the same. The bicycle was propped against the wall and the shelves were neatly stacked apart from one cardboard box left on the workbench that seemed to contain different cords, ropes and elastic ties. A few other items cluttered the space.

The constable's radio burst into life. "Go ahead."

"According to the electoral roll, he lives alone. No known police record."

"Thanks."

They opened the door at the back of the garage that led into the garden. A small patio filled the space. Some rusting metal chairs leaned on the round table. Grass was growing through the gaps in the flags. "Not a gardener then!"

April smiled.

The garden area was large in comparison to the size of the house. Mature trees formed a boundary to two sides; an open fence bordered the field at the bottom. A structure, that could have been a large shed or summerhouse, was positioned near the far end of what could loosely be described as a lawn. Net curtains covered the windows.

"I'll check this if you wander over and look around the trees just in case he's collapsed there."

April frowned and followed the instructions as the PC put his hand against the glass and tried to see inside before moving to the door. It was locked.

He turned to April. "Please see if there's a key in the garage or the kitchen for this place." He watched as she re-entered the garage. He walked around the back of the structure, stopped immediately before taking two steps backwards. He fumbled for his radio. "Control, 633. Fast paramedic. Immediate request."

April came into the garden carrying a key on a long string. She noted the expression on her colleague's face. He pointed to behind the building.

"No wonder he couldn't make your meeting. He's here."

Chapter Nineteen

Cyril and Owen walked up the path to the vicarage. Tape fluttered along the fence and across the road, dissecting the main thoroughfare through Clipton. The central area was isolated but a few inquisitive spectators were already hovering on the periphery. The officer stood at the door and directed Cyril and Owen around the side of the building in order to maintain the integrity of the house, pending the arrival of a full forensics team.

"He's where he was found, sir."

A screen had been erected on the drive. A forensic tent allowed both Cyril and Owen privacy when donning the necessary plastic overshoes, suits and gloves before moving towards the summerhouse. A temporary screen had been built shielding the corpse from the open farmland at the rear of the property. The Reverend Ian Fella hung from the large hook that was secured to the timber frame. A rope dug into his deformed neck. A short distance away from his feet was a tumbled stepladder.

Owen noticed his clothing first. "He's dressed in red."

"It's a convocational robe, a red chimere. Now that's unusual as they're originally meant for bishops." Cyril looked carefully at the way the noose bit into the flesh of Ian's neck and made a mental note.

The officer who accompanied them suddenly spoke. "He's got something in his hand, sir, but we can't see all of it. It's screwed up tightly. Looks like a piece of paper."

Owen moved more closely, careful to position his feet on the step plates that had been placed to protect the scene.

Cyril called out a warning. "The plastic plates are slippery when wet. Seen many a copper come a cropper."

Owen lifted his hand in acknowledgement and moved with great delicacy for a big man. He wanted to see if he could determine what the vicar was holding but moved away quickly; as with all hangings the bowels of the deceased had opened. "We'll wait." He lifted his hand to his nose.

Cyril could not help but smile. "You returned faster than you went. Lesson learned, Owen, lesson learned."

"Still very pungent, sir. Makes you wonder why a man of the cloth would take his own life. He always seemed such a happy man, involved in so many community activities," the attending officer said as he moved a little further away, already aware of the stench.

Owen turned to the officer. "How well did you know him?"

"As I said, he gets involved in a lot of community stuff. I take a local youth football team and he likes to come along. Gets quite worked up, wears a team-coloured scarf and always brings a football rattle, belonged to his father he told me. The kids loved it. When was the last time you saw one of those?"

Owen looked at Cyril with a puzzled expression.

"Like the old police rattle, popular post-war with football supporters until they were banned in the 1970s. Used them as weapons." Cyril then turned to the officer. "When was the last time you saw him?"

"Sunday at church, my wife's in the choir. I help out as a sidesman. He was fine. In very positive spirits."

"This might seem like an odd question considering the circumstances..." Cyril turned his head and looked at the hanging figure and then back to the officer. "Do you remember the theme of his sermon last Sunday?"

There was a long pause. "To be honest, I wasn't really listening, the wife'll know."

"I'd appreciate a call when you find out." Cyril smiled.

Two Crime Scene Investigators vans arrived in support of the first and as the investigators unpacked, Cyril and Owen moved away. Caner, the pathologist, unfolded a blue, plastic sheet and placed his case onto it.

"Cyril, Owen." Caner smiled and nodded to each. "Dr Pritchett tells me that you have a head for heights when it comes to a post mortem, Owen. Not many officers like the cut and thrust do they, Cyril?" He smiled at Owen. "I'm impressed."

Owen returned the smile, more out of shock. He had always considered Caner to be a miserable old bugger devoid of any personality or warmth. Now he was seeing a different side to his character.

"I don't even carve the Sunday roast, Isaac, and I like my steak well done, no blood," Cyril said and gave Owen a wink. "We'll leave you to it, please give me an approximate time of death when you can."

Dr Caner nodded, this time the smile was absent. "As soon as."

Cyril and Owen stripped off their protective clothing and deposited it within the clinical waste bin on the edge of the crime scene.

"May I ask a question, sir?"

Cyril paused and looked at Owen.

"Have you always had a fear of bodily fluids?"

"When I was a nipper my mother took me on a day trip to Southport, father was working. We boarded the coach early morning and we set off along windy, country roads like the proverbial bat out of hell. Despite protestations from the passengers, the driver seemed determined to get there before we'd set off. Halfway through the journey I was feeling decidedly grim but luckily we pulled up at a roadside café for a toilet and coffee stop. We were near the back and the passengers were moving more slowly than the contents of my stomach. My mother just managed to hold out the shopping bag containing our packed lunch and I exploded into it as well as covering the front of my clothing. As I'd no spares, I spent the rest of the day feeling decidedly ill with the continuous smell of vomit hitting my nostrils. Never really got over it. As you know, I still don't travel well as a passenger when being driven at speed. As for blood, Owen, that story can wait. Now look, the vultures have gathered."

Cyril noticed that the local press had already arrived, recognising a young lady standing by the tape. He walked over and had a quiet word, assuring her that a full statement would be made in due course. He then ducked back under the tape and moved towards the cars that were trapped within the two bands of police tape. April was sitting in her car working on an iPad.

"You okay?" Cyril asked leaning on the car roof.

She looked up and smiled. "It's not the first time that I've found a body but I always hope that it might be the last."

Cyril paused respectfully, understanding full well how she was feeling before responding. "Nothing prepares you for such a discovery. April, take Owen and go and chat with the lady you spoke to earlier this morning. See if Fella was acting differently recently, you know the routine; I don't need to say anything about the sensitivity of the situation do I?" Cyril looked at both of them.

***

Dr Caner was waiting by the gate to the vicarage, his bag resting on the fence. Cyril approached as April's car pulled away from the kerb. An officer lifted the tape to allow its egress.

"Four hours at most. Although the ambient temperature is low, the body was overly dressed and so it's only a rough estimate. My profession is, Cyril, after all, a blend of art and science, it's a delicate balance of je ne sais quoi!" He paused momentarily. "What I should say from what I've seen, however, is that you're not looking for anyone else involved directly with the hanging. Whatever is in his hand will stay there until we get him on the table. I take it Owen will attend?"

Cyril smiled. "Why train a good dog and then bark yourself, Isaac?" He brought to mind his initial meeting with Ian

105

Fella and pondered on their conversation. He did not seem to be a man who was unduly stressed or worried and certainly not a man who would consider taking his own life. He appeared contented with his lot. Cyril then reflected on the dangling corpse, thinking about the tightly held note. He was sure that Caner was wrong, but then, what did he know?

A black van was allowed through the cordon. It quickly reversed onto the driveway as directed with minimum fuss and maximum discretion. The screens were swiftly moved to the front of it before the gurney was slid from the rear. The wheels suddenly dropped as if it were an aircraft about to land. It was then trundled into the garage and the door was closed. Cyril climbed into his car and headed for Newby Wiske.

***

April knocked on the door and Ralph replied with a long, low bark. She turned to Owen. "Ralph!"

Mrs Fleet opened the door and on seeing April, smiled. "You again and you've brought a handsome young man with you."

April lifted her warrant card and introduced Owen who was still smiling from the compliment. "May we come in?"

"I'll just put Ralph in the yard. Please wait there." Mrs Fleet closed the door.

"Is that a dog or a donkey?" Owen asked.

"That's Ralph."

The door was then opened fully and they were shown into the conservatory at the back of the house. Ralph was sitting just outside the French windows.

"He's a good dog, likes females but unsure when he's around bonny young men." She smiled at Owen. "Nothing personal you'll understand. Must have been badly treated as a pup. He's a rescue dog."

Owen lifted his hand.

April was quick to respond. "How was Ralph with Reverend Fella?"

Mrs Fleet turned and looked at the dog and then back at her. "You haven't met Ian have you? I said he didn't like bonny young men. If you had you'd understand. He was fine, Ralph liked him; mind Ian always brings him a pig's ear every time he visits." The smile disappeared as quickly as it had come and Mrs Fleet looked April squarely in the eye. "What are you really getting at and what's this all about? Something's happened, hasn't it? I knew that when you left so rudely this morning. I could tell that you were keeping something from me."

April ignored the comment but continued with her questions. "Mrs Fleet, how well did you know Reverend Fella?"

Both officers watched Mrs Fleet's expression closely.

"He's been the vicar in the area for a number of years, involved here, next door. We've known each other for ages and we've worked together for a long time. We're both very committed to the church." The last part of the sentence faded to become almost inaudible. After a short, uncomfortable pause, she asked April. "What's happened? Please tell me Ian's all right."

"I'm sorry to tell you that Ian Fella was found dead this morning. I cannot tell you more, I'm sorry."

There was a long silence as Mrs Fleet put her hand swiftly to her mouth. She shook her head, clearly shocked by what she had just heard. "I know he sounded ill when he rang but I'd never have guessed he was so ill. Goodness me."

She held the chair arm and sat down. Her face was ashen. At the same time a tear streamed down her cheek. Ralph moved closer to the window and barked as if sensing his owner's emotional trauma.

"I'll put the kettle on. You need a warm drink." April stood and went through to the kitchen. Ralph watched her every move and barked a second time. Mrs Fleet placed her hand reassuringly on the glass door.

Chapter Twenty

Cyril turned off the road onto the driveway at Newby Wisk, the North Yorkshire Police Headquarters. He had been coming there a long time but that was to change. Soon it was to be a centre for adventure holidays for children and their teachers after the recent sale of the site. He paused and admired the beauty of the building. He knew Alveston Court in Northallerton, the new, purpose-built headquarters, would be a better centre, more able to deal with modern day policing but he was still saddened by the imminent move. He smiled to himself as he wondered how the Chief Constable's desk would be transferred. He knew it as the Eiger, a mountain of papers, a personal filing system that was horizontal and secured by different pebbles and rocks.

The Chief Constable's secretary greeted Cyril like an old friend.

"You're looking well, Cyril. A spring in your step too I see."

Cyril kissed her on the cheek. "Thank you, busy but then…" He didn't finish as the large mahogany door opened and the Chief Constable approached. There was no hint of a smile.

"Proverbial hit the fan with the alleged racist attack in your neck of the woods, Cyril, and now I believe we have a suicide, an established member of the Christian and broader community. Let's hope that they don't come in threes, not with all of this going on." He raised his hands as if in despair. "Come!" He turned and walked back through the large doors. Cyril looked at the secretary who pulled a face as Cyril raised his eyebrows. "To the lion's den." He quickly followed.

"I'll bring coffee, that will help calm troubled waters, usually does."

"The Reverend Ian Fella, fifty-four. Unmarried, been at Clipton for some time also involved in the local smaller churches and communities. He was also in the forces as a young man, Falklands War veteran, Marine, mentioned in despatches. Took to the church after his service. Tell me why you were there today. I read in your report that you visited him a short time ago." The Chief Constable looked down at some notes he had made that were lodged on the edge of the heavily laden desk before returning his attention to Cyril. "Have we disturbed a hornets' nest? Considering some of the goings on, what with discovering Christian symbols left around Harrogate, now these two incidents falling so closely together and showing clear signs of being linked, doesn't look like a coincidence to me, Cyril."

Cyril spread his hands. "Routine enquiries regarding Gideon Fletcher, it's all on file. Fella was the last to see Fletcher before he disappeared. However, we have a strong suspicion that he's returned or that someone is using his past and his connection with the past as some kind of cover. We had the initial link to Fletcher from the discovery of dyed hair attached to crosses and that led to my interviewing Fella. However, that brought its own questions after we were told of Fletcher's final words to the vicar."

The Chief Constable invited Cyril to look at a computer screen that had been facing away from them. Cyril stared at an image of one of the wooden crosses, not dissimilar to those found in Harrogate and held by forensics. He slipped on his glasses before dipping into his pocket for his notebook. He cross-referenced the number on the screen with those held.

"This is the type of cross..." He paused and turned. "We don't have this cross. The ones we hold were discovered with links to Gideon and a missing female. The link, as you know, was in the DNA of the hair sealed within the attached packets. We hold crosses marked 12, 1, 13, 9, 8 and 6 and now this, number 5."

"Found with Reverend Fella, it was in an envelope in the house hidden in a locked drawer. Attached was a biblical reference."

"*Though your sins be as scarlet, they shall be as white as snow; though they be red like crimson, they shall be as wool,*" Cyril interrupted.

The Chief Constable smiled. "Indeed, Cyril, astute as usual but also there was this hand written section beneath, *Like Rahab all Christians have a scarlet cord hanging in the window of their souls…* We received these images and details ten minutes ago."

The secretary brought in the coffee and left it on a side table. Only Cyril acknowledged her with a nod. Cyril returned his gaze to the photograph as it appeared on screen.

"April Richmond, a temp DC from Leeds, who's working the case has an astonishing biblical knowledge. She's a Sunday school teacher, and she linked the numbers on the crosses to thirteen human weaknesses." Cyril reopened his notebook, turned the pages and read from the list. "Taken from St Mark. I've made notes." He flicked to the correct page of his notebook. "Jesus mentions thirteen things that defile a person: *For from within, out of the heart of men, proceed evil thoughts, adulteries, fornications, murders, thefts, covetousness, wickedness, deceit, lasciviousness, an evil eye, blasphemy, pride, foolishness.* It is a supposition at present that the numbers written and scratched on the crosses are in some way linked, so if we take those in order, we have one to thirteen."

Cyril handed over his notebook.

"If that were the case then we can assume that the number on the cross refers to theft, providing, that is, that the perpetrator is working to the same list and the same order."

"They're ordered that way in the Bible but yes, supposition as I said, but we can't rule anything out at this stage. We'll see what the pathologist finds but Caner was adamant that it was suicide and if that's the case then maybe someone or something has pushed him over the edge."

"So why have the other crosses just been dumped, left without any consideration as to whether they'd be discovered?"

"If you take them in the order you see there and compare the numbers, I think that we're all guilty of those weaknesses; evil thoughts and foolishness and others. I have to hold my hand up. Maybe whoever left the one at the vicarage didn't anticipate Fella taking his own life. Maybe it was just a warning to him that someone knew what he was up to. It might even reference something historical."

"Anything at the scene of the acid attack other than the human hair?"

"As yet no but we're searching Kumar's business premises and home."

"The case is in safe hands. I'm sure that you're keen to get back. Keep me informed, Cyril."

Cyril looked at the pot of coffee and realised a drink would not now be offered.

Chapter Twenty-One

Shakti and April were in the Incident Room when Cyril returned. Smirthwaite busied himself on one of the many computers alongside other officers who were dealing with the reports and information that had come in from the various public appeals for information. The social media posts had garnered a number of enquiries and each had to be checked and verified.

Caner had requested that Owen attend while the paper was extricated from Ian Fella's hand.

"Sir, Caner has managed to extract the paper and we have another cross location."

Cyril placed his coat over the back of a chair and moved quickly to April who pointed to a whiteboard. A photograph of the wrinkled paper was clear to see and in the middle of the page were the words, *Including you!* The photograph was attached to the board by four magnetic discs. Cyril moved more closely and straightened the disc ensuring that they were all symmetrical. He noted too that the handwriting was marked in red ink. "Fella told us that. They were the last words Gideon uttered as he left the night he disappeared, the same night he'd had a meal with Ian Fella."

April looked at Cyril. "Mrs Fleet was clearly shocked when we went to see her. She believed that he was poorly but not seriously ill. I suppose that she never considered his mental state and neither did she ask. As far as she was concerned he was his usual self."

"Was there anything going on between them?" Cyril asked eager to know more about the cross that had been found.

April smiled. "I spoke with Owen after the visit and as far as we could tell, nothing unless someone has witnessed an indiscretion or she tells us then..."

"Open mind on that one then. How's she now?"

"Distraught to be honest. Her sister's coming over for a couple of days, lives in Beverley."

Cyril nodded. "The cross?"

It was clear from her expression that Shakti was eager to tell. "Mada was speaking with Mrs Kumar about their house move and their plans for the future. It's been difficult. Mrs Kumar's been surrounded by members of her family since her husband's death. That's normal believe me. This morning Mada showed her a photograph of one of the crosses we found and immediately she realised that she'd struck a chord. It turns out that when they moved in to the new property, a similar cross like that was found in the garden when they were having it landscaped and planted. The gardener brought it in and her husband couldn't understand how it had ended up on their plot. Prophetically she believed it to be a harbinger of bad luck. It was, as far as she can remember, damaged by the gardener's spade. One of the arms on the cross piece had broken."

"What happened to it?"

"Abdul, her husband, put it in the bin."

"Bin?"

"It doesn't end there. Fortunately and unbeknownst to her husband and remembering that she was fearful but respectful of the find, she wished to get rid of the piece appropriately. She mentioned to Mada that one of her relatives fought with the British in the First World War and she felt as though it shouldn't be in the bin. She took it and placed it on the Grove Road Methodist Church War Memorial when she was passing. She told Mada that she didn't want to put it near the Cenotaph, as it's usually too busy. This, however, was a couple of weeks ago. We've sent a car to see if it's still there. Heard nothing as yet."

"Anyone like to guess the number that's on it? That's if there is a number."

All eyes glanced at the list of human weaknesses that were clear to see on the board. A phone rang and Smirthwaite answered the call. He listened and then covered the mouthpiece turning to Cyril. "It's there. Some damage."

"Number?" Cyril asked impatiently.

"Scratched mark that looks like a number three."

Cyril smiled at April. "We have a match! It looks as though your theory stands up to scrutiny too. We can go with that but still with a degree of caution. Well done all. Thank goodness for Family Liaison Officers."

Owen came in, his jacket slung over his shoulder and his finger in the loop.

"Someone looks happy," Owen said looking at Shakti.

"Owen, the waters appear to be getting muddier not clearer." Cyril quickly explained what had occurred that morning before Stuart Park chipped in.

"Why three and not two?" he asked. "Surely he committed adultery. These biblical terms can be so bloody confusing."

April looked at Owen and smiled. Even though he had come in on the end of the discussion, Owen did not need a second prompt.

"In biblical terms, adultery is when an unmarried man has sex with a married or betrothed woman whereas number three, fornication, means when a married man has sex with an unmarried woman and therefore we can assume that whatever went on in the car on Brimham Moor was between him and..." Owen tossed his jacket onto the table.

Stuart Park nodded. "Right, thanks!"

Owen turned to April and smiled.

Cyril put his hand on Owen's shoulder. "Good man! Been doing your scripture studies, I see, as well as your anatomical work." Cyril took Owen to one side. "Now, how was April after leaving the vicarage?"

"Strong, sir. Works really well." He blushed wondering if Cyril had guessed that April had furnished him with his newfound biblical understanding.

Cyril patted him on the back. "What time's the autopsy?"

Owen checked his watch. "Another couple of hours. Looking forward to it."

"A brew in ten would be lovely. You've time." He smiled at Owen. "Dry saucer is your challenge." Cyril collected his coat and went to his office.

***

He was on the phone when Owen entered. The cup rattled in the saucer as he lumbered through the door, his tongue protruding through his teeth as he concentrated on not spilling a drop; he was successful. Cyril lifted a hand in thanks and pointed to a chair at the other side of his desk. Owen sat as Cyril continued with the call. He let his eyes drift around Cyril's office; it was always impeccable, just like him really. He glanced at the top of the filing cabinet and noticed that Liz's photograph had been removed. He looked back at Cyril with a degree of concern. Since her death he had always had the photograph there. Cyril was watching him closely. He finished the conversation.

"Mada on the phone." He picked up the cup and saucer and sipped the tea. "Good brew as always, Owen. I noticed that you were looking for Liz?"

He nodded. "The photo's gone." He pulled a strange face that suggested a degree of embarrassment and curiosity.

"She's still here, Owen. She comes and goes as she pleases now you could say."

Owen really did not have a clue as to what he was talking about but simply smiled, uncertain as to how he should deal with the situation. He knew that Cyril had been through some dark times but on the whole looking at the man you would not notice it.

He drained the cup and rested it on the saucer. "What information should we be chasing, Owen, after our conversation earlier?"

115

Owen looked at Cyril. "We need to know who the gardener is who found the cross at Kumar's house."

"Ten out of ten, Owen." Cyril leaned on his desk. "Interestingly, I was just speaking to Mada. She tells me that the gardeners for the site are contracted to the builder. The site foreman was somewhat surprised; no gardener had been allocated to Kumar's address on the day that the cross was discovered. They weren't due to sort Kumar's garden for another week according to the builder's schedule. I've asked Mada to talk to Mrs Kumar and get a description; she has with her the photographs of Gideon so we should soon know if she's had a visit from the missing Gideon Fletcher. If that's the case, then we can safely assume the murder was pre-meditated. Kumar was set up."

Cyril looked at his watch. "You need to go, you have an appointment with Caner."

Owen looked at his watch. One minute. "If we have crosses definitely linked to theft and fornication that in turn are linked with deaths representing those sins, if I can use that term, what others might not apply to the general man in the street? Can we just forget about the ones that were left around?" Owen stood seemingly a little more comfortable with his newfound knowledge.

"They all apply, Owen, that's the tricky bit. What constitutes sexual immorality to one individual might not to another whereas theft, adultery and fornication are pretty clear-cut. The grey areas I believe at this stage of the game we could put to one side as you rightly say. What we must do now is concentrate on the black and white. We have potential for more victims if we don't track down Gideon. Interestingly a report has come through regarding Ian Fella's last sermon. Turns out to be modern day temptation. Spoke about instant gratification that today's society seems to need, the lack of patience and tolerance. He also mentioned false news. I've asked to see if there's a draft on his computer. Might prove valuable. I'll get April to chase that up."

Chapter Twenty-Two

Owen stood momentarily on his toes as he peered down at the three people working around Ian Fella's naked body. He was used to the cloying atmosphere that seemed to hit you physically. He could never quite put his finger on it; even though the temperature appeared fine he always seemed to feel uncomfortably hot. It could be nerves or maybe it was just him.

He concentrated on the corpse that seemed vulnerably exposed, only then did he recall Mrs Fleet's words, *You've not met Ian, have you?* Here he was broken and in some ways undignified; the rope lay on a small side table. The reddened flesh at the lower part of the body seemed in stark contrast to the upper part of the torso.

Caner talked his way through the removal of the thoracic and abdominal organs before handing them over to an assistant. They were weighed and their general condition noted before being moved to a further work station for a more detailed analysis. To Owen, the room suddenly seemed brighter than usual and he could feel the perspiration bead along his forehead. He took a deep breath but kept his eyes focused on Caner and his colleagues.

"We'll be moving to the neck shortly, blood and tissue samples will be screened. Toxicology results shouldn't take too long. Are you all right?"

Owen just smiled and waved a hand, thankful of the glass screen that separated them. Somehow he felt more secure than being in the same space.

"Why the blackening to the neck?"

"There are a number of types of hanging; this one was a slow one, a strangulation. It was painful I'm afraid and probably quite prolonged. Looking at some of the damage to the

117

elbows and heels there was a degree of severe thrashing of these limbs against the building's surface. Scratch marks to the neck here and here, you will see them clearly on the screen, suggest he had second thoughts and tried to ease the pressure on the neck and allow air passage, but once the steps had been removed he had little hope, unless of course, the rope or hook had given way. That could account for the greater movement but my experience tells me that in strangulations you tend to find the body squirms and fights. The blackening to the skin is due to the heat caused by friction of the ligature. You'll notice here that displacement was to the right owing to that movement..."

Owen heard the words decorticate and decerebrate rigidity but they passed well over his head. He was focussed on the man and not the body. He wondered what could drive someone to go through that. What could they have done that required such a devastating and undignified end? Surely nothing is more frightening than tying a rope around your neck and then kicking away the only means of staying alive.

"... Fracture of the thyroid and hyoid, normal considering the age of the victim. They ossify. We know that there was a fixed knot rather than a slip, and the noose was just large enough for the head but then very slack around the neck. We observe a transverse tear to the carotid artery. If you look at the screen you can see it clearly."

Feeling a little more composed, Owen looked across. He was finding the terminology interesting but confusing. Caner paused; all the while photographs were being taken. The team performed like clockwork but on occasion Caner wanted specific and more detailed shots.

"You're doing well, Owen, not long now. However, we'll not have toxicology for a while. I told Cyril that I was convinced that there was nobody else involved." Caner stopped and stood back from the table before looking directly at Owen. "Considering the damage to the elbows as I mentioned before and the ligature marks here and here on the skull, I now feel that others might have been involved. This man tried to release the

118

rope whilst he thrashed. How did he maintain the grasp of the note?"

Owen's ears pricked up. "So there's a chance he was murdered?"

Caner lifted his Perspex visor and looked at what remained of Ian Fella. "I'll need to do more tests and see the results of the fingernail samples but I'll say on record that this was not a suicide. The note was added at the point of or just before death. I don't believe he would have placed it in his own hand."

Owen removed a screwed-up tissue from his pocket. The observation window, even though it was angled, misted slightly in the area directly in front of him as he leaned forward. He wiped the window and then his brow. "When will you know?"

"Give me six to twelve hours and I'll give you a definitive answer. Well done again. Seeing Hannah must be good for your constitution!"

Owen smiled as the picture of Hannah swam into his mind. He could not argue with that.

***

Graham Baker sat across from his wife. The aroma of the freshly prepared meal lingered. He sipped from his wine glass as she finished the last part of her dinner.

"You'd been saving that until the end." He knew how much she enjoyed the chicken wrapped in Parma ham, and she had left a small mouthful on the edge of her plate.

She looked up and smiled. "You prepare it so well, darling." She lifted her glass. "To the chef, cheers!" She moved her glass towards Graham's who quickly reciprocated.

"A pleasure as always."

"After working in the garden it's so good to come in to a beautiful meal. You've been out early the last few mornings. I hear you but I feel so tired."

119

"It's all the fresh air you get from gardening and shopping. I only wish I could do more."

"You do enough. I had a dream the other night that I saw you leave, heard the garage door and saw the car lights..."

"Maybe we should not have wine with our evening meal, love!" He laughed.

"At my age? I'll risk it!"

Graham poured her another glass. "Thought I might have heard more from the police. I bet they're not interested in finding the poor woman. They're more interested in showing their happy side at Pride marches and such. Did you see them at Notting Hill prancing about? Supposedly keeping the peace, at one with the general public, instead they're messing about performing the Samba with some semi-naked girl who seems to be sprouting feathers from every orifice! Meanwhile someone is being beaten to death half a mile away. They tolerate some disgusting behaviour, frightened of being seen as party poopers, that's what it is. They've lost all respect; nobody is frightened of their teachers or the police nowadays. Even the church bends towards a weaker society rather than having society grow and develop towards those demands made by the church. I've said it before and I'll say it again, everyone's got to be frightened of someone or something otherwise you'll have anarchy... We have anarchy what am I saying?"

He took two tablets from his pocket, popped them from the packet and swallowed them with a mouthful of wine.

"You had your tablets this morning, dear."

He just raised his eyebrows and mumbled some obscenity.

She sipped her wine and smiled. "Here endeth the first and only lesson. It's a good job you can't get onto a soap box otherwise I'd buy you one for your birthday." She chuckled to herself. "You're like a record player, dear."

Graham stood and crashed the empty plates together. "If there was more discipline, more rigour, society would be a lot more stable, you mark my words. I'll wash up. Shopping tomorrow?" Graham asked, his voice now less strident as he carried two stacked plates into the kitchen using a stick to help guide him.

"Felicity said she'd pick you up and drop you in town as usual. I'll do the cleaning and I've ironing to do." She watched his slow progress to the door. "I'm sure you could manage without those things, it's just confidence, that's all. You've come to rely on them too much. Remember what the specialist said?"

He stopped not making the manoeuvre to turn and confront her but from the tone of his voice, she could gauge his facial expression. "Yes, yes but he doesn't have the spine I have, he doesn't understand the pain I'm constantly in. The sticks give me support, keep the pressure away and with that the pain and discomfort." He disappeared through the door, ending the conversation.

"You haven't drunk your wine." She looked at the level in both glasses. Graham had only had a sip or two. Glancing towards the door, she quickly swapped them. Graham smiled.

121

Chapter Twenty-Three

Cyril had arrived at work earlier than usual. He had one or two loose ends to try to sort out for other members of his team working on another case.

April sat in the Incident Room, a large sheet of white paper in front of her. Owen came in after he had uploaded his report.

"I'm glad you're here, April. Murder and not suicide, Flash said so if you remember. He's bloody good."

"Flash?"

"I'll tell you some other time. It's his nickname but whatever you do don't let him hear you utter it, he'll have your guts for garters!"

"My nan used to say that." She chuckled. "So what made them change their minds regarding Fella?"

"Caner just said that now he was convinced that it wasn't suicide and that he'd know definitely tomorrow after running more tests. They're amazing really what they can discern from the smallest of clues. I've texted Cyril. He'll be delighted that he was right. May I run something past you? I've been having a think. It's about the Bible sayings, not the thirteen weaknesses but the ones you and Cyril picked up from Fella."

"Happy to. How can I help?"

Owen looked at the photograph of the Telfer Pyramid gravestone that was situated within Clipton churchyard. "Your report stated that when we were talking to Ian Fella he mentioned about Rahab. He also mentioned that Gideon had revealed that he came to the pyramid for correction, it was where he heard the voice of God. He was adamant that it was where God corrected him. I found that quite disturbing when I read it."

122

April nodded. "Yes. There's something about the story of Rahab and that of Gideon Fletcher that have remarkable similarities."

Owen removed a pen from his pocket and prepared to jot down his thoughts on the large sheet in front of him. "May I?"

April smiled.

"I did some reading but I'm not sure if I've got things right. Fella said that both Rahab and Gideon had similar stories. Both were, and I quote here from something I read about Rahab, *on the dunghill and then placed with the gods.* You learn all sorts in this game, April! Rahab was a harlot, in Hebrew a Zoonah and in Greek the word is Porne, from the latter you see why she was a bad 'un like our Gideon. I'm sure you're aware of his past and how suddenly when in prison he had a Damascus moment. Anyway, I digress, sorry."

"Her home was in the walls of Jericho and when Joshua was preparing to attack the city, he sent two spies to check out the military strength. However, they were compromised and they went to the inn run by Rahab. She realised that they were men of God and needed a favour, a different favour from that asked by men who normally entered her inn. It's believed also that she dyed yarn and the spies hid under a pile of yarn that was drying on the roof to escape their pursuers. They used a scarlet dyed rope to escape.

"It was promised that once the city was captured, she and her family would be freed and spared from death if there were to be a massacre. The sign they should hang in their window should be a red cord. When the attack took place, all those homes with the scarlet thread hanging in the window were spared. It's said that this may be the reason brothels have a scarlet lamp hanging outside but I can't possibly say."

April observed as Owen completed his notes, impressed by his diligent research. He then brought the pen to his lips.

"So, Owen, changing character from bad to good is one connection that they share and then the scarlet cord linking the crosses and the dyed hair that have been found. But why hair and not just plain old thread?" She watched his eyes scan the notes before he tapped the pen against his teeth. "And why is he drawing us to Rahab in the first place?"

Owen lifted a finger and then smiled. He then wrote in block capital letters, *HAIR HAS A DNA TO TRACK AND WE'RE LOOKING FOR OUR OWN RAHAB.*

It was April's turn to pull a face as she looked across the broad expanse of paper. Hesitantly she said, "He's set us a trail?"

Owen nodded. "Firstly, we need to look at the Telfer Pyramid again and we need twenty-four-hour surveillance on that site. If God is still correcting him then he's still returning. Come on, enough for one day."

April looked at Owen and although he had the reputation of not being as good a copper as Cyril she could see why they made a perfect partnership.

They both stood. Owen checked his watch. "Tomorrow at 07.30. I'll check if any CCTV images from the Clipton area have come through. I put out a request to the public for any dash-cam images in and around Clipton and the church that show a single person who might be deemed suspect." He held up his hand. "A massive stab in the dark I hear you thinking but we have to grasp at straws occasionally. There's also the footage from houses near the church and the vicarage. We're checking constantly the local ANPRs too. We can soon eliminate the neighbours."

"Gideon might live in the area!"

Owen stared at April. "Further house-to-house with Gideon's picture once suicide has definitely been ruled out. Don't work too late. I'll phone Cyril first thing and let him know what we're doing. See you tomorrow." Owen left.

***

April moved through to the general office. The collection of desks and the computer stations sat empty. Shakti was the only officer left at her desk. She looked up and smiled as April approached.

"I'm so pleased you're still here. I've been meaning to speak to you for a while about the missing woman, Tracy Phillips. What exactly do we know of her past? I've read the reports and know she was working at the Oak Hotel but what about prior?"

Shakti flicked onto another tab on her computer and brought up the file. "It's all here, you've read it. Still nothing."

"Just chatting with Owen and we've both come to a similar conclusion that we could be looking for a woman who might and I use the word carefully, might be connected in some way to both murder cases. We know that she was identified in the DNA taken from the hair trapped within one of the packets. What we need to do is find out if at any time she was a harlot."

"A what?" Shakti could not help but laugh. "So you mean a whore? A prostitute?"

"Both mean the same so I guess you got it in one." April rested her hand on Shakti's shoulder. "That's the answer we need right now."

April moved to her desk, pushed out the chair and sat back. She felt the buzz of adrenalin, an excitement she had longed for since joining the force. Here working with Cyril and his team she felt accepted. She glanced across at Owen's desk, a battlefield of chaos, and smiled. She had realised just how valuable he was within the department and she felt proud that he had come to her for advice. She returned her glance to the computer screen to the right of her desk, it was black but attached to the edge was a Post-it note on which she'd written, 'Socialised and Integrated Psychopath... NOW!' It was the last thing she needed. She looked at her watch before the screen turned blue and the crest of the North Yorkshire Police hit her squarely in the eye.

Chapter Twenty-Four

Cyril had been home for an hour. He had polished his shoes, shaved and changed. The invitation to dine at Julie's had been welcome. Although he always had a feeling of excitement when visiting, on this occasion it was tempered by his need to confess something of his past, a past that he liked to keep hidden and private. He had hoped that he could share the contents of the letter he had received sooner but there had never seemed to be an appropriate opportunity. He acknowledged that there had also been a certain reluctance on his part. It had been bottled up for so long he had wondered whether she or anyone else needed to know, after all, it was nobody's business but his. Somehow, for a reason he could not truly fathom, the arrival of the letter had prompted a sudden need to share his past with someone very close and on this occasion, Owen was not even in the frame. After careful consideration, it could only be Julie.

***

Julie had a sixth sense regarding Cyril's sudden moods and she knew that he was keeping something from her or that work was beginning to prove too distracting for him. Could the ghost of Liz be affecting his judgement? The therapist had certainly warned Cyril that Liz's presence might remain within him as another voice, a presence that might either control or invade his imagination at stressful times. The latter was the more concerning. She let her thoughts linger a while longer until she considered a more dangerous scenario. Maybe, April, the new temporary officer, was playing on his mind a little too much. He had been referring to her more lately and his mood seemed to be lighter when she was brought into the conversation. At that thought, Julie laughed but only to herself, more out of uncertainty than anything else. It was, on her part, whistling in the dark confidence. She then felt foolish for her jealous thoughts. In reality, she knew that she could never totally discard the possibility; after all, Cyril was a handsome man, probably impossible to live with permanently, but nevertheless worthy of a fight if one were needed.

***

The evening was still chilly but it was fine and Cyril had decided to walk, to do what he did each morning to focus his thoughts. He needed a way to approach the implications of the letter to Julie and the subject of his past. He was far from feeling comfortable as he walked up the pathway before glancing at the blinds shielding the lounge bay window. The anxiety was reminiscent of the time that he was waiting for the doctor's discharge that would signal that he could return to work after Liz's murder; the same heavy-footed butterflies were there, the slight nausea and the feeling of helplessness. At least on this occasion his future was not in someone else's hands, it was definitely in his. The thought made him remove his hands from his pockets. He stood for a moment and looked at them before clenching his fists. At least here, at Julie's, things remained the same, he could relax and if the time proved right he would tell her. "Time!" He said out loud. If the letter were accurate, time was certainly not on his side.

He knew that once he had rung the bell the blinds would open, her smiling face would appear and all would be well. He unclenched his left fist and rang the bell, turning to watch for the flicker of the blinds but he was surprised to hear the immediate click of the electric catch on the door. He frowned and his heart sank. He pushed open the door and entered. Thankfully the hallway had not changed. He glanced at the flowers on the narrow table, the black and white tiled floor. "At least you're in the right bloody house, Bennett!" He could not resist walking to the end of the hallway and glancing at the stained-glass window on the landing. The streetlights seemed to give it a special, nocturnal magic. The door to Julie's apartment was ajar.

"It's open!" Julie's voice sang out from deep within before echoing in the hallway.

A flush of nerves fluttered briefly in his stomach as he pushed open the door. He removed his shoes placing them, as always, to the side. He looked around the room and noticed the glass of red wine waiting next to the chair he favoured. The recognisable tones of Guy Garvey could only bring a smile of pleasure. The ambience was perfect and Cyril immediately began to feel his shoulders relax.

"You know me too well, Julie Pritchett," he said removing his coat before following his nose into the kitchen. Julie was by the stove, a blue and white striped apron round her waist. "Smells divine."

He moved behind her and kissed her neck. "And so do you young lady, so do you!"

She dipped a spoon into the saucepan and turned to Cyril proffering the steaming taster. Her free hand was held beneath to catch any drops. Cyril instinctively blew on the offering before sampling the sauce.

"I've always loved gruel!" His impudence earned him a slap on the arm.

"Pearls before swine. Pork Veronique, I'll have you know, duchess potatoes and green beans for me. For you?" She paused holding a finger in front of her face. "Soup... I have a tin somewhere, probably out of date and full of *Clostridium botulinum*, an ingredient that should not only cure your sense of humour but might well help with your wrinkles." She jabbed playfully at his eyes with two spread fingers before tossing the spoon into the water in the sink.

Cyril laughed. "May I help?"

"You can leave me in peace. It'll be ten minutes." She kissed his crow's feet. "There, a kiss to make them better, laughing boy."

***

Music from a live band drifted out over Montpellier Hill from one of the bars, the occasional laugh erupting above it, briefly attracting the stare of the solitary figure sitting on the bench that was almost hidden in the gardens. The large hood of her coat was drawn over her head, creating a dark cavern that concealed her face. Wisps of cigarette smoke were occasionally exhaled to drift lazily into the surrounding gloom.

Her voice, low and melancholy, was almost robotic. "He doesn't want fucking much! *I'm doing as I'm told!* he says. Jesus he's a grown fucking man. *Not long now!* he says again and then again." The cigarette butt was ejected with a spit that showed her anger. It travelled to the right of the bench before hitting the path causing it to flare and die. "He thinks there's only him that has needs. What about my fucking needs? He says we've to do this, we've to do that. Fuck me! He's not the only one telling me what to fucking do. What about him in here?" She jabbed her right temple. "And him here?" She swapped hands and jabbed the left side of her head. "They all want me to do this and fucking that! Want, want, want fucking want!"

She wrapped her arms around her body and tucked her legs under her on the bench as if to make herself invisible. "I'm going to tell them, tell them once and for all to just fuck off and let me lead my own life."

She removed a hand and felt for money in her back pocket. It was empty. A low growl erupted from within the hood. She heard the voice whisper and she immediately responded and chewed her lip. The voice came again and she obeyed, biting harder before sucking the wound and releasing the metallic taste to linger on her tongue. "Fuck all this for a game of soldiers! Fuck! I hate this." She stood and screamed at the

129

top of her voice, "Fuck you!" The last word rang out for a few seconds ejected along with the fine mist of minute, bloody globuled saliva. A man started to run towards her.

"Are you all right?" he called in all innocence and with great concern as he approached. When he saw the solitary hooded figure standing in the shadows, he stopped. He watched as she raised her arm and pointed a finger at him as if it were a gun.

"Stop just where you are. Fuck off! I don't need your fucking help. I don't need anyone's help. I just want all this chattering to stop!" She turned and ran towards the darkness of The Stray. All the while an observer standing within the shadows of the gardens had witnessed everything. He simply crossed himself and smiled.

Chapter Twenty-Five

Cyril stared across at Julie as she finished her meal.

"Are you going to leave that last incy wincy duchess potato, Detective Chief Inspector Creosote?" She adopted a French style accent mimicking a Monty Python sketch that they both loved. For Cyril it was said at the wrong moment as his mouth was full of red wine. He struggled to keep himself from spraying the potato and the surrounding area. Two red, liquid lines dribbled from the corner of his mouth and down to his chin before he quickly caught them with his napkin.

"Cut! You're supposed to explode after you've eaten it remember."

He laughed again.

"Take two!" She put her hands together and opened them like a clapperboard before changing their shape to mimic a movie camera as she brought them to her face pretending she was now filming.

Once he had regained his composure he leaned over and collected the potato. "Beautiful meal. Thank you."

Julie allowed the pause in conversation to linger longer than normal before she asked. "What do you want to talk to me about, Cyril?"

Cyril nearly choked again. He looked across the table.

"Cyril, I know you. Something has been eating away at you recently. You're not the only one with detective skills. It's called intuition and women have it in bucket loads." She stretched out her hand and rested it on his reassuringly.

Cyril felt in his breast pocket, withdrew the envelope and handed it to her. "I'll go through to the lounge whilst you read that. There's no rush and no need to comment but I'd appreciate it if you give it some thought." He collected the bottle of red wine, topped up Julie's glass and went through to the lounge. He felt his anxiety return.

***

Within five minutes, she came in and leaned over to kiss him on the head. "Why didn't you tell me about this before?" She sat opposite.

"It's always made me so angry, Julie. The past, him, her, the way someone's trust can be so badly and cynically abused." He sipped some more wine as if trying to find the courage for which he was searching further down the glass. "I knew about it when I was too young, too frightened and too naïve to tackle the situation. My silence seemed to signify and to suggest my acceptance when what I should have done was refused to tolerate what I could see was clearly going on. I should have stayed at home and not been forced off to boarding school, protected her especially when she started with her illness. I should have fought my mother's corner, but then, I knew nothing of the onset of her illness, that was kept from me until it was too late. The information I received as a child was extremely doctored and besides, at that age I had little say in any domestic matters." Cyril paused and stared into his glass. "And when I was old enough it was too late."

The letter had given a brief and almost apologetic potted family history. "How did you know your father was having an affair?" Julie's tone was measured.

"During a summer holiday I'd gone to the local airfield to watch the aircraft land and take off. You could get right under the flight path. I'd cycled there. I remember it as if it were yesterday. I'd gone because I'd heard that the de Havilland Mosquito was going to land there. Christ was I excited to see it!" Cyril paused as if replaying the memory.

For the first time, Julie saw the child in Cyril's eyes, she could see the pools of vulnerability and innocence that she knew

132

would soon be sullied and felt a flush of love for the vulnerable man sitting before her.

"Goodness, Julie, when it took off and flew above me no higher than this ceiling, the Merlin engines at full chat, I wept, I tell you. I took two photographs on my Fuji Instax, an instant camera so that I could relive the moment immediately the plane had disappeared over the horizon. There were no digital cameras then. Excitedly I started the journey home, eager to tell all who'd listen about the Mossie. Cycling was a pleasure and I was, in my mind at least, flying home, not cycling, making all the accompanying aircraft noises. Any German car seen was a clear target for my imaginary guns. I didn't shoot down many." He laughed out loud at the memory.

Suddenly his facial expression changed. "It was then that I saw him, my father or should I say my father's car. He had an immaculate maroon Bentley, you'd never miss it. It wasn't new, more a classic, but he used it every day. It was down a farm track. Innocently I thought I'd get a lift home but there was no one in the car. Leaning my bike against the hedge I went to see if everything was all right. It might've been a Bentley but there was more than one occasion when it came home on the back of a recovery truck. I heard before I saw. The animalistic sounds quite frightened me, especially the female's high-pitched gasps. Sounded as though she'd hurt herself." He looked at Julie. "As I said, I was young and naïve. Only when I saw them did I realise what was going on. She was on all fours and he was behind. Both had their eyes closed but I could see them clearly. I realised it wasn't Mum, it was one of her closest friends. Why I took the photograph I don't know, probably because my camera was with me, around my neck. I don't know. That day was suddenly sullied, shot to pieces, a maelstrom of confusion. I remember the torment in my mind as I cycled home oblivious to my surroundings."

"Was that this Wendy?" Julie held up the letter.

Cyril nodded and topped up his glass again. "I put the camera away, never used it again that summer. The

133

photograph, I just kept looking at the photograph. I hid it and then I took it with me back to boarding school. It was later that same summer I found out that Mum was ill. Within a year she'd be dead. Mum was nursed at home for as long as possible. It was only later did I discover that Wendy came and stayed at our house to look after her as Dad was working. She had cancer nurses coming in but she refused to leave. I believe that she knew what was going on and in some ways, considering my mother's kind-hearted nature, she probably condoned his behaviour believing in her heart that my father wouldn't cope with being alone." He looked up, his focus indeterminable. "She knew more, she probably thought that I'd need a mother, that she wouldn't be there for me. That was the type of woman and mother she was, she always put others before herself. It was so brave of her, so very brave."

Cyril downed the remaining wine in the glass, went to the cabinet and poured a brandy. He was so immersed in the past that he ignored Julie. It was as if she were not there. He appeared to be talking to the past about the past. She said nothing.

"The only consolation for me," he continued, "was that he waited a respectable period of time after Mum's passing before he married Wendy. The whole thing challenged for me my perception of relationships, of man and wife, of love and marriage." He mumbled afterwards, "Go together like a horse and carriage." His mumbling stopped. "Why? Why make the commitment? Why promise this and that? I couldn't wait to leave home. I resented her, Wendy, my stepmother, she was the bitch, the schemer, she was my father's bit on the side, my mother's so-called best friend. Even though she tried to be kind to me I despised her.

"After this I couldn't wait to return to school, to get away from those who'd betrayed my mother. It was when I was away that I spoke with my housemaster. He could see that I was a troubled soul and I told him everything. It was only much later did I find out that my father had been to see him so that he was fully aware of my circumstances. However, my housemaster was sensitive and told me a story and it's that story that brought total confusion and made me truly think about fate and coincidence, to discern fact from fiction. Maybe, the very reason, the very point in my life where I was determined to become a copper."

Julie stood, collected the brandy bottle and poured herself a glass before topping up Cyril's. She sensitively touched the two glasses together, smiled at Cyril and settled down without uttering a word.

"You saw the envelope?"

Julie smiled. "Cyril V Bennett. A man with a secret!" Two words immediately sprang to mind, victorious and valiant and as quickly two words replaced them, vulnerable and victim.

"Vaughan," he paused. "… after my mother's favourite composer, Ralph Vaughan Williams. My mother was a violinist, a very good one too. She'd for me as far back as I can remember until she was too ill to play but then she'd listen to music. Fantasia was her favourite, The Lark Ascending mine; I see her face every time I hear it. It's usually a bittersweet moment, Julie." He paused and hung his head.

Julie knew better than to interrupt, to break the moment of reflection.

"She even tried to teach me… hell's bells… I proved to be as musical as a stone trough." He laughed briefly breaking the heart-searching for a welcome moment. "That's not the story but you needed to know that; without that information nothing else would make any sense. The housemaster told me that Vaughan Williams was happily married and later fell in love with a much younger, married woman, forty years his junior. When Vaughan Williams's wife fell ill, his lover helped nurse her and as a consequence she became close friends with his ailing wife. The scenario was almost identical. The only difference, Julie, that's critical in this, Vaughan Williams had no children to torment mentally with his tangled relationships."

"Torment, Cyril?"

135

"Torment, mental angst, confusion, add whatever title you want. It's the questions, questions that can never be answered that are the worst. Questions I failed to ask my father. He became the man I despised then and the man I despise now. Did my mother know this about Vaughan Williams's life? Surely yes, without a doubt. Did my father meet Wendy Swann before I was born? I don't know. Did the knowledge of my father's illicit relationship bring about my mother's illness? I can't answer that. Did my mother condone the relationship so that I might have the security of a mother's love when she passed away? I'll never truly know, Julie, but I'm sure all this turmoil has plagued my life and my relationships with women, has made me the man you see today, good or bad. It's made me the career copper, a Detective Chief Inspector, hopefully good at his job, but it's also made me the man who shuns permanent, personal commitment just in case…"

She put her glass on the table. Kneeling before him she took both his hands and kissed each tenderly. A tear rolled down her cheek. "I'm so sorry to hear about your father. Wendy says the doctor has given him three weeks at most." She squeezed his hands. "It's so kind of her to find you and tell you so that you have time to make a decision. You are, my darling man, who you are, made up of a plethora of parts. Your parents are only a small element of the complex person you now are. You hold your mother's memory close and so you should, she wanted the very best for her boy as any mother would. If she could see the Cyril Vaughan Bennett that I see and know, she would be an immensely proud mother, just as proud as I am, knowing you and loving you." Julie turned his hands over and kissed his palms. "I love you, Cyril Vaughan Bennett and don't you ever forget that."

Chapter Twenty-Six

Cyril's phone vibrated and danced across the bedside table until it crashed in the void between the bed and the table. His uncoordinated, searching hand failed to stop its Icarus flight. He pulled himself onto one elbow and the pounding in either temple suddenly attracted more attention than the phone. Leaning down he managed to retrieve it.

"Bennett," he announced with a whimper.

"Good morning, sir. Lovely morning."

Cyril had not yet managed to open his eyes fully. He had tried but even the semi-darkness proved to be a hurdle. All he felt were the hammers pounding above his eye. "Owen." He moved the phone away from his ear. Owen sounded far too loud and far too jovial.

"Well done, sir. You received my text?" There was a long silence.

"Text?" Cyril groaned trying to comprehend what Owen was talking about.

"You were right about Fella. Caner is convinced it's not suicide just as you thought. Beautiful morning. It's so good when the sun shines and..." He failed to finish.

"Owen, I don't want a weather forecast. Is everything all right?"

"I've had a thought."

Cyril groaned. "I've warned you about those before. Have a brew and it'll pass." Cyril hung up. His head crashed back onto the pillow. Even with his eyes closed the room seemed to be rotating. The phone vibrated again.

"What do you want, Owen? It's the middle of the night."

"It's just past eight, sir, according to my watch but then it's only a cheap, plastic digital. Just letting you know I'll be in Clipton until about eleven."

It was Owen's turn to hang up abruptly. He turned to April who was driving. "Bloody bear with a sore head today. Not like him at all. Let's hope he's found his inner calm before we get back."

April turned and smiled. "He always seems so measured, so in control."

"He can't have got out of bed on the wrong side as I'm sure he was still in his pit... or Julie's!" He turned and winked at her. "Remember, April, careless talk costs lives." She giggled.

***

The churchyard was quiet. "No Grim Reaper this morning?"

"What?" Owen asked as he watched the wet grass soak through the front of his shoes.

"When I was here last time I was surprised to see a woman cutting the grass using a scythe, made me think of the Grim Reaper."

Owen plodded on mumbling something about wet socks. He had failed to respond; why should he? She had assumed correctly that he had no religious belief, only a fleeting, professional curiosity about Christianity and he would, she believed, only be interested in enough to help solve this case. He looked at the church clock. Just after eight-thirty. "Where's the pyramid grave?"

"Beautiful church, Owen."

He turned and looked at her. "It's lumps of stone, one on top of the other. Does nothing for me apart from tell the time."

April pointed in the general direction whilst admiring the trees' resplendent mantle, a fresh, clean green that contrasted vividly with a small, grey cloud that was the only imperfection in a blue sky. It puzzled her as to why it should be there, an imposter, but then she looked at Owen crossing a grave with little respect and could not help but see a similarity.

"Now that's different!" Owen said with a newfound burst of enthusiasm. "If you want to mark your last place on earth then that's how to do it. Mind, the old pharaohs' tombs rather put this to shame but then this is Yorkshire where pennies are counted, unlike the Egyptians who got theirs built for free. Wonder if there are funerary objects and a sarcophagus beneath our feet, maybe wealth beyond our wildest dreams?" He turned to look at April who stood nearby, a face that revealed enough for him to refocus his thoughts. "You're right, probably not. That photograph on the board doesn't do it justice. If you look, the grass has been trodden quite heavily around the base." He believed that if Gideon continued to visit there would be some clue. "What do we know about it?"

"The vicar told me that they get a lot of visitors to see it." April opened her notes. "Grave of Thomas Telfer married to Elizabeth known as Bessie. He was an explorer, engineer and architect. He inherited a fortune from his father and they travelled the world. He had a keen interest in all things Egyptian. He wrote a book on his interpretation of how the great Giza pyramids were constructed."

Owen walked around looking carefully for any marks that might appear new or anything concealed within the moss-covered edifice. He stopped, his eye drawn to some missing mortar between courses of stone. He quickly knelt and looked into the dark void. There was nothing. His disappointment was palpable. He stood and let his eyes wander around the churchyard. In the far corner, Owen spotted a large mesh bin, more a compost heap than a general dump he realised after closer inspection. He wandered over and as he did, April moved and inspected the pyramid grave.

***

Julie brought a glass of water and two paracetamol tablets. Cyril was hidden beneath one of the pillows, his hands folded across the top.

"I thought that considering you consumed most of the brandy last night, you might need these. I take it that was Owen on the phone earlier?"

Cyril groaned.

"You can't be a man at night and a little boy in the morning." Julie laughed, conscious to begin the day on a brighter note than the nadir that had ensued the previous evening. No conclusion had been reached as to whether Cyril would visit his father but considering the body language that he had exhibited and his frame of mind, she doubted it. She knew how stubborn he could be. "It's your day off. It's my day off. You can't stay in bed all morning."

Cyril's hand shot out and grabbed Julie's arm. "There could be a worse fate."

Julie screamed as she fell across him and then giggled.

**

Owen looked carefully at the many bunches of brown and withered flowers, all testaments to the sheer grief of losing a loved one. The only colour evident was the occasional ribbon and written card. Owen read a few, *Sweet dreams my dearest sister, Always remembered, Until we meet...* He picked up a branch that lay by the wall and lifted the upper layer.

April also looked into the crevice between the courses of stone and like Owen, she too was disappointed. She moved the grass from around the base to inspect the bottom course of stone. Her eye was drawn to something concealed by the corner.

"April!" Owen's shout made her jump. "What do you make of this?"

She straightened and walked over to Owen who was standing by a large bin. He was holding what looked like a

140

branch inserted into the pile of rubbish. She turned her head sideways and searched the area near the tip of the branch. There were two cards on which personal sentiments had been written. The recent rain and their location had taken its toll; the writing was smudged and the ink had leached into the card, blurring the script. He noted that none of the cards had the protective covering that he had seen on those positioned on the graves. Owen observed that it had had the desired effect on April. She suddenly became rigid and stepped back before pointing at the card. She looked at Owen but before she could say anything Owen nodded.

She read the card out loud.

Tracy Phillips 20 May, - 3 June 2017.
When shadows fall and death hides you from the world, you will walk in sunshine.

"Surely a coincidence, not the missing woman." April read it again.

"What have you missed?" Owen's voice was calm and reassuring. It was clear that the name on the card had caused a degree of confusion.

She read it again.

"Look at the dates," instructed Owen.

Her hand moved slowly to her mouth. "Today's date is..." She checked her mobile, "... the seventeenth of May." She felt a shiver course throughout her body as the facts slowly hit home.

"Photograph it, please. We must find your Mrs Reaper and have a chat. We need to know where this particular note was left but somehow I doubt she'll know. If this isn't a hoax then sand in Tracy's timer is fast running out."

They both took photographs of the card's location. "Don't touch anything else. Call it in. I want Forensics to go through this lot and check. We don't know what's at the bottom of this pile." He lifted his eyebrows. "Let's just not miss a trick here. Get them to close off the churchyard whilst they check."

April suddenly remembered. "I thought there was something by the pyramid." Turning quickly, she ran back to the point around which she'd been searching. She moved away the grass and the soil. Owen bobbed down beside her.

"What have you found?"

"I thought…" She used the end of a pen to pull more soil away. "… A stone!" She exclaimed, clearly frustrated and very disappointed.

"Ring Shakti and send her the picture of the find," Owen called as he made his way towards the church porch; April followed. He looked at the public notice board; discoloured cork tiles covered with different notices. April took out her mobile phone and photographed it before reading the notices. Owen found what he was looking for. In the corner in a sealed, transparent bag was a list of people connected with the church and their telephone numbers. "Bingo!" he muttered as he started dialling. On the third call, he found her and after a brief conversation was given the address of the local gravedigger who tended the church grounds. Owen stepped outside the porch to get his bearings.

He smiled at April. "Come on, we're going to have a chat with a gravedigger. I knew they had them in the past but today, with all the technology, I thought they'd bring in one of those mini diggers."

The sound of an incoming message caused April to check her phone; it was a message from Shakti. "Do you want her to contact Cyril?"

"Yes, but we don't need him in, just keep him informed."

Chapter Twenty-Seven

The rustic, brick cottage belonging to John Barlow was just round the corner from the church. The heavy, oak door sat within a small porch. The light still cast a yellow glow into the eaves even though it had been daylight for a number of hours. Cobwebs were strung from the fitting to the wooden beams that formed the roof's structure. Owen let the knocker crash against the metal plate. Within moments the door opened. Owen was taken aback. For some reason he had expected an elderly man, skin like old leather and hands the size of shovels. He was temporarily lost for words.

"Mr Barlow?"

"And you are?" Barlow appeared to be in his mid thirties, of average height and build.

"DS Owen and DC Richmond." He held up his warrant card. "Do you have a minute?"

"If it's about Ian I've already spoken to a local officer, a lady, can't recall her name. Also chatted with our local copper, member of our church. He's really shaken. Seems to have affected him after the event. I believe he found him." Barlow showed them in before taking a seat in the lounge. "How can I help? Can't believe it really. Ian was such a jovial chap. He was always willing to help with a word or a favour. We never know the true workings of the human mind. Strange thing, the mind, we can't close it off. I sometimes question my sanity. I'm surrounded by the dead, I work amongst them, sometimes even find myself talking to them!" He shook his head. "Never any arguments though."

Owen smiled. "So your job is to manage the graveyard, Mr Barlow?"

"Aye, amongst other things."

143

"Apart from Reverend Fella's death, we're investigating the disappearance of a woman from the Harrogate area about eighteen months ago. You might recall it was on the TV and in the press. Whilst checking round the graveyard today we came across this in the waste pile where the dead flowers are cleared to." He held April's phone so that Barlow could see the card. "I know this might seem like a silly question but do you remember where that bunch of flowers was placed originally?"

Barlow laughed. "I doubt it." He studied the photograph and then looked at Owen and then April. "Tracy Phillips, no, sorry. Don't recall a Phillips buried here. It's a quiet churchyard. Sometimes I read the cards and on other days, particularly if it's been raining, I don't I just put them on the compost."

"Do you work by hand? Digging graves, I mean?" Owen's earlier curiosity got the better of him.

"I work in churchyards locally where it's impossible to bring in machines to dig. My job used to be known as Church Sexton in the past encompassed many things including grave digging but now you seldom hear the title. My role is to make sure that everything's looked after and no one nicks the lead off the roof and when the need arises, dig the odd grave. The pay's poor but this cottage comes with the job. I look after three churches and it suits me."

Owen pointed again at the photograph of the card.

"Sorry, yes." He studied it again. "Yes! I remember now, that bunch of flowers wasn't put on a grave. It was found in the porch one evening when I was doing my walk round. The flowers were already dead as if they'd just been dumped. I know kids didn't put them there, we get very little trouble from the local youth as we have an active sports community. I also checked with the two ladies who help with the grass cutting but they didn't see anyone."

"When was this?"

Barlow rubbed his chin. "I'd say about a week to ten days ago at most. I compost the flowers and keep the paper but the other bits, plastic and the like get put in the general waste bin."

"How often is it emptied?"

"The mesh bin? It's not now. Used to be, we sent it to the local tip but now, as I've said, we separate anything that's not degradable and then leave it to rot down. Once it'd composted, parishioners could come and take it. I'd bag it and a note would go on the church's Facebook page and in the magazine. Ian wanted the church to become as green as possible. As well as saving souls, he was into saving the planet. He set areas aside for butterflies and wild flowers. We've even got a hedgehog house."

"So that's not been touched since...?"

"I'll not be drawing compost from the base until August once the rain and the sun have done their job."

"I'm sure you were asked this when the officer spoke with you after Ian Fella's death but have you seen anyone coming regularly to the churchyard, someone who isn't a church goer?"

"We've some who tend the graves of loved ones. Some come yearly, I believe, whilst one comes monthly, another weekly. Old Mrs Mortimer comes every day. Walks up the path, pops a biscuit on her husband's headstone and leaves. The birds come immediately, seem to know the time. He was an ornithologist, lovely man. If the truth be known, I think he got Ian into this eco- friendly frame of mind. I know what you're thinking, if you mean the mysterious and slightly bonkers Gideon chap, no, I've never seen him. Heard the stories but I've never seen him. Dressed like Jesus, I believe, and gave out pages from the Bible to anyone he saw. Takes all kinds I suppose. Ian told me to keep an eye out for him."

"Can you show us the graves attended by the three regular visitors?" Owen informed him that there would be some police activity at the church.

***

A blue and white tape closed off part of the churchyard and a small forensic team was in the process of setting up. Barlow showed them the three graves, all relatively new. April photographed each one for reference.

Owen thanked him and walked over to the second tape to observe the forensics team. The compost bin had been flanked on two sides by white tarpaulin sheets and the masked and hooded figures worked methodically, photographing and stripping layer after layer of detritus from within the mesh cage. Even when it had been spread on one of the sheets, more photographs were taken and notes made. Once the pile was reduced by a third, the front top section of the mesh container was removed using snips to allow easier access. It was then that he saw one CSI pause. Two of the investigators moved closer. They had found something. A CSI holding a camera walked on the step plates away from the immediate area of the bin and then towards Owen. She pulled at her mask until it hung round her throat.

"Thought you'd like to see this," she said holding the rear screen of the camera towards Owen. "That's the back. The front's facing down." She flicked onto the next image.

Owen could clearly identify it as a Remembrance cross, possibly in worse condition than any they had found to-date. It was attached to a small plastic bag that was so encrusted that it was difficult to see whether or not it contained human hair. He studied the cross trying to look for a number but partly rotted vegetation had adhered to the wood owing to the constant compression of the pile. He knew that if there was no number on it when they retrieved it then it might have been left on a grave on Remembrance Sunday.

"Is there a chance of removing some of the crap when you get it out? I need to see if there's a number on the front."

The investigator walked back and spoke with one of her colleagues. She turned, looked at Owen, gave a thumbs up sign and then spread her fingers as if to signify, in five minutes. Owen suddenly felt both nervous and excited. If there was a number on the cross then there was a higher chance that something or someone might be at the bottom of the pile. He had had a feeling about the pyramid and the churchyard and it looked as though following his gut instinct was paying off.

The cross was finally extricated from the layers and passed to someone kneeling over a fresh, white sheet. It was again photographed and then brushed. Layers of rotting, wet vegetation flaked reluctantly from the damp wood. Owing to the colouration from the compost and the compression, the timber had taken on a similar hue to the vegetation camouflaging the wood, making it difficult to see if anything had been written or scratched on it. The CSI dug into a box and brought out what looked like a low-light, filtered torch and a hand lens. Holding the cross at an oblique angle, the yellow light was shone across the wood's surface. Owen watched with great interest. As the lens and torch went back into the box, butterflies erupted in Owen's stomach. The CSI bagged the cross and the attached bag, stood and approached Owen.

"It seems there might be a numeral just below the cross section. I can't be sure at this stage owing to the damage but it may well be a number seven. There might be human hair within the attached packet but until we get it into the lab that's the best we can do. Sorry, must get on." He turned but suddenly looked back. "What I will say is that this heap has been disturbed relatively recently. It's been dismantled in large sections and then put back. The boss thinks there might be something at the bottom."

Owen thanked him and took out his notebook looking for the references he had made regarding the thirteen weaknesses. "Seven was linked to wickedness."

The CSI looked puzzled, smiled politely before walking back towards the site. He placed the bagged find into a storage container.

April approached and Owen explained what had been discovered. She turned and looked back at Barlow who was leaning on the wall. "He's been asking a good number of questions, seems a little nervous."

"To be expected. We're on his patch, he'll feel responsible if anything's discovered and if it is, April, he'll feel even more hot under the collar because in old copper speak, I'll be feeling it. "Can you let Cyril know? He might just want to be here if they find something else, or, heaven forbid, a body turns up."

***

Within an hour the mesh compost holder had been cleared. It did not have a base. Each corner of the large cage had an extended spike that anchored it to the ground. Owen was leaning on a gravestone. He had cupped his eyes with the palms of his hands and was giving them a rub.

"Sir!"

Owen was startled. She had called him *sir* which was the equivalent to his granny calling him *David* when he had misbehaved. "What's up?"

"They're bringing screens. They were clearing a layer of soil, then suddenly they all stopped simultaneously."

"Let's hope it's not Tracy Phillips."

The photographer came over again. "Naked female. We've called for backup, the police doctor and additional support. It looks as though it's going to be a long day."

***

Within the hour, Cyril had arrived wearing his aviator-style sunglasses. He walked steadily towards them before removing the glasses. Owen could not fail to notice two things, firstly the dark shadows beneath his eyes and secondly that he was carrying a bottle of water. It was not like Cyril at all. Owen had seen the dark shadows before, but water! He said nothing, thinking it more diplomatic to wait for Cyril to open the conversation.

"Where's the gravedigger?"

"Barlow, sir. John Barlow." April pointed in the general direction of his cottage.

"Show me. It's going to be a long day, Owen."

"Second time I've heard that." He pulled a smile across his lips.

"What brought you here today?" Cyril asked with genuine curiosity.

"Gut instinct, sir, gut instinct."

"Good man. A good copper knows when to follow what his instinct tells him" He paused turning to April. "There's a lesson to learn, young lady. Owen here is one of the best. Learn from him whilst you're with us."

Chapter Twenty-Eight

Graham Baker waved one of his sticks as he watched his daughter-in-law, Felicity, drive towards the roundabout by The Crown Hotel. He stood momentarily admiring the array of flowers within the island. He walked up the pathway to find an empty bench that was in the sunshine.

Within minutes, he was settled. He rested his sticks against the edge of the bench, removed a book from his coat pocket and relaxed.

***

Cyril woke early and felt much brighter than he had the previous day. Just being with Owen had not helped. Copious glasses of water and paracetamol had got him through the day. What he needed was his routine walk to work to ensure that any lingering cobwebs had been blown away.

On arrival he went to his office, opened the bottom drawer and looked at Liz's photograph. "You'd have loved this mixed-up muddle of a murder inquiry, DS Graydon. I wonder if you know from where you rest?"

He smiled and slowly slid the drawer closed. Standing outside the Incident Room he noted that there were a considerable number of his team chatting whilst waiting for the morning briefing. The discovery of the named card, the cross and the human remains had created quite a buzz. Two officers leaned against the wall, files tucked under their arms. One was pointing to a photograph he held in his hand. The intensity on their faces clearly showed the significance of the find. As if a switch had been thrown, the noise stopped and all eyes followed Cyril as he entered and approached the chair that had been

150

readied. People moved to their respective desks or propped themselves on a nearby table. Owen shuffled the papers in front of him. April, to his left, had hers stacked and ordered. Shakti was next to her.

"Morning, thanks everyone." He looked up and scanned the room. "You've all had an opportunity to see the latest information that's come to light. The body found buried below the compost bin in the churchyard is that of the missing girl, Angela Rhodes; known to her friends as Angie. Mother reported her missing over a week ago but this isn't the first instance she's gone missing. We've had a number of reports of her absence over the years, particularly during her schooling. Mother's a known and registered addict, and Angela was taken into care when she was very young but caused so much disruption and walked out on so many occasions to return to Mum that it was felt that's where she should stay. It appeared to be the best move for the child at that point. I'm sure there'll be a review about that decision somewhere. She was assessed at one stage and the psychiatrist's report is in your file."

"9c," Shakti stated.

Cyril lifted his hand in thanks. "She clearly exhibited signs of psychopathic tendencies, in particular the self-harm and her destructive nature. It was felt that this was brought about by the mother's heavy drug taking during pregnancy. She was born an addict with serious developing mental issues. She was with a foster carer for a good six months before she was given back to the mother despite a number of concerns from professionals involved. According to the report, there have been some domestic issues with neighbours but nothing serious. All in all, this girl hadn't a lot going for her from the start. Father has not been on the scene since she was born."

"We did receive complaints from neighbours that the home was a knocking shop but there was nothing ever found to substantiate the allegations. Social Services were again involved to monitor the girl's welfare but once she turned eighteen there was nothing they could do. We've had no recent

151

complaints but whether mum and daughter were prostituting themselves we cannot tell. All I'll say is that the mother was extremely concerned that her daughter had been missing for more than four days as she's aware that she's dabbled in huffing glue and taking other illegal highs in the past. The mother was extremely concerned she'd overdose or whatever you do with these things."

"Prophetic," Smirthwaite grumbled.

"For a period of time, she worked in a local factory that produces sauces but was asked to leave after she was caught urinating into one of the vats. Let's say that she was a very troubled young lady. Report suggests that she's been dead for about six days. She died away from where the body was discovered so must have been transported. At this stage we cannot rule out murder, owing to the discovery of the cross. The body was naked when discovered but no evidence of sexual interference. Cause of death was diagnosed as aspiration of her own vomit." There was a silence as those in the room contemplated the thought.

"Terrible death, terrible!" someone murmured.

"Considering that the cross, the same as the ones we have, was found with her it's another murder, surely?" Stuart Park was swift to ask.

Cyril continued. "The girl was found in a shallow grave in a foetal position. The cross was placed within the compost stack just above her, attached to which was the usual bag of scarlet, dyed hair. According to Forensics it contained two DNA samples, one was that of the dead girl but the other has yet to be traced. The cross was marked with a number 7."

Officers sifted through their files for the relevant photographs.

"Why, who and when, Stuart? It seems to me that the substance that killed her, according to the report, was amyl nitrate. She was huffing. From the post mortem results, it's clear she's been an abuser for some time but on this occasion the particular inhalant was either modified or stronger than the norm. Whether she was forced to inhale it we don't know. It's the why. Why has someone linked this body with Tracy Phillips's card?"

"Sir!" An officer near the back interrupted.

Cyril pointed.

"Reading through this case it doesn't really make any sense. We've discovered crosses, human hair that's been tracked to different individuals, most of whom are missing. There's only one we know who isn't and that's Kumar's wife. We now have three bodies. My question is why? Why this charade? Nobody's gaining anything. This girl died about the same time as the vicar, that's if my maths is correct, give or take a day."

"Firstly, serial killers don't work to any forms of logic…" Cyril tried to recall the officer's name.

"Mason, sir. Callum Mason."

"Yes, sorry, Callum. In my opinion this isn't about revenge, it's not some wanton act, it's about correction. Correcting their weakness, putting them out of their misery. It's stated that Gideon went to that churchyard, to the pyramid grave not to hear God speak but to receive correction. Now whether that was to receive personal correction or orders from a voice in his head to do some correcting… we don't know but what I do know is that it's now our job to stop this foolishness as quickly as possible. And yes, both died about the same time."

Cyril knew what the officer was thinking and quickly came back. "Are you thinking one might have been involved in the other's death?"

Callum nodded. "I hadn't ruled it out."

"We'll have to keep an open mind on that."

Owen took over the briefing. "Consider the date of death shown on the card found in the bin and the two murders. You've noted that Pathology has serious doubts about their initial interpretation of the evidence to suggest that Fella committed suicide, that Tracy Phillips's life may well be in danger. Our job is to find her before that date."

A number of hands sprang up and Cyril paused, pointing to one officer.

"How do we know it's not a hoax, someone messing about? If you think of all the resources channelled into an investigation like this, it leaves us exposed elsewhere, sir."

Cyril looked at Owen and then back at the officer. "I'm very much aware of the cost implication, Harris, and to answer your question, we don't, but what we do know is that we have three bodies connected in some way to that graveyard. Those are clearly not coincidences they are facts. We started with two people missing Gideon Fletcher and Tracy Phillips. We now have three dead and a third connection to the missing woman, the first connection being the hair DNA, the second the discovery of the newspaper and the note, and now we have this, the card. What we can speculate is that all of this appears to be down to one man, Gideon Fletcher. Owen?"

"We've brought in John Barlow, the gravedigger, for questioning and we're researching his background. He informed us that he originally found the flowers and the card not on a grave but in the church porch. We have four CCTV images and a dash cam video that is on file and you should all have seen this. They are poor quality and the tech people are still trying to enhance them but this is reality if you like and we can't perform the miracles that you see on the television dramas!"

There was a slight chuckle.

"Now, if you look at the images of the card found you can see the dates and the handwritten note. Significantly, everything else in this case, other than the note found within the newspaper handed in by the public, has some biblical reference. This note didn't but it contained the words, *When shadows fall and death hides you from the world, you will walk in sunshine.*"

Smirthwaite commented. "She's not going to die if you read that. When we think she's dead, on that date, she'll be in sunshine. The Costa del Sol, no doubt!"

His flippant attempt at a joke fell flat. Cyril made a note to have a word with him after the briefing; he was an experienced copper and he expected a more professional approach.

It was Shakti's turn to get involved. "Interestingly from the twentieth of May to the third of June is exactly thirteen days! Coincidence?"

Cyril looked up when he heard the word and a slight flutter hit his stomach.

She continued. "We have two references to shadows now too." She fumbled through her paperwork. "Here it is. Remember the note we received wrapped in the newspaper? It stated *...she just stopped walking these streets, a shadow of her former self.* And then here we have, *when shadows fall...* Is there a connection?"

Cyril noted her comments. "Thanks. Could there be a chance that our Gideon could be Tracy Phillips?"

He watched as a number of heads turned and a degree of chatter broke out. He let it continue for five minutes until they had all discussed Cyril's idea. "After all, they've been the two missing people from the outset and they're still missing. The floor is open for your thoughts."

"Could she, Angie, be the person in the back of Kumar's car, our very own Rahab?" Stuart Park chipped in. "Or could Angie Rhodes have been in the car and this is her reward for knowing too much? You did say that there was a chance she was a prostitute."

April raised her hand just to show she wanted to speak.

"April?" Cyril's voice quietened the room.

She stood up and went to a blank whiteboard. "This has been on my mind for a while after speaking with Reverend Fella but your words earlier about Gideon hearing voices makes it even more relevant, I think." She sounded nervous and looked to Owen for an encouraging nod. "I've had a note attached to my computer to research something that we all studied when training, some of us anyway, but for me it obviously went in one ear and out of the other and so I had to look it up."

This self-deprecation helped others feel a little more comfortable. She wrote SOCIALISED AND INTEGRATED PSYCHOPATH.

"When I first heard about Gideon Fletcher this came into my head. I had an inkling of an idea about these evil characters but I couldn't remember the small print. The more I read, the more I realised we were looking for a chameleon, someone who blends perfectly into his or her surroundings. I read that one per cent of the population fits the profile of a psychopath but we are looking for a much rarer beast. This individual is truly evil and manipulative."

She looked around the room and realised that the title had suddenly produced light bulb moments in a number of her colleagues. "They're dangerous primarily because they're hidden. People don't expect friends, lovers, people in authority to do them harm or to be so evil. They're skilled at managing what people think about them. They're very intelligent, form relationships, trusting relationships easily and from there, their reign of abuse begins. Interestingly, sir..." She looked at Cyril. "... in the list I read it suggested that dominance over individuals can lead to sexual and physical abuse, emotional and mental abuse and theft. It's my opinion that we are looking for a chameleon, a manipulator and tormentor. From what I know about Gideon, he was far from that in either of his guises. He's an utter thug and criminal, someone who stood out from the crowd. However, there's something there and I'd welcome your thoughts."

It was Mada who quickly responded. "Sorry but no, April. Gideon isn't a chameleon. The chameleon analogy is misleading. Remember the famous saying, if you want to hide something, you hide it right under their noses. Gideon could have believed that. People trusted him, saw him regularly, and he was always the same, particularly in his later guise when he was recognised by his clothing and his familiar wave.

"When I was a kid at school a teacher told a story of a sheep thief who was caught. In those days they branded him on the forehead with the letters ST. He was ridiculed and no one trusted him and so he went away and was determined to change his ways. Years went by and all he did was good deeds and although he wasn't fully accepted because of the letters branded on his face, over time, people did begin to trust him. It was one child who asked what the letters S and T stood for. The adults were themselves unsure and thought for a while. One suddenly said, 'This man is always so kind that they must stand for saint.'" There was silence. "People accepted the changed Gideon, his past was soon forgotten but as April says, the voices he heard were still there just routing him along a more sinister path."

"Good point, Mada," Cyril said but then noticed a slight flush to April's cheeks. "Vital information, April. Notes everyone and read up. Okay I now want to go off on a relevant tangent. You should've all read that the call to Mrs Fleet on the day Ian Fella went missing was made from his own mobile. The phone records have not thrown up anything of interest or untoward other than that fact and there's no way we'll know who made the call. Forensics has gone over it but again nothing unusual.

"Shakti. I want you to come with me to interview Mrs Rhodes. Owen and April... Barlow. He can have legal representation later. Caution him but he's not under arrest. You know the drill."

***

Graham Baker had not been particularly engrossed in his book. The sun warmed him and although he had only been there for thirty minutes, he felt a little sleepy. The early mornings were clearly catching up with him.

The figure looked down from the road. Even though there was a garden between them, Graham's sideways, slumping body could clearly be seen. Graham felt the seat flex as someone sat next to him and he opened his eyes. He turned to see who it was. A smile crossed his face and then a frown.

"Sam? I thought..."

"The delivery girl. She's gone. No more early mornings, Graham. No more collections. If I ever need you again I'll call."

"What about my packets? You can't just stop."

"I can and I will. Goodbye, Graham."

***

Cyril quickly allocated tasks to the team and emphasised the need to get their findings uploaded as soon as possible. It would be a small discovery that would make all the difference he emphasised.

"I'll be ten minutes, Shakti."

Everyone started to disperse. He turned to Mada. "How's Mrs Kumar?"

"Surprisingly good. She's managed to get rid of the family members that had encamped with her and life seems to be back to normal. We've not found any evidence to implicate his professional business colleagues with any impropriety. How far back his inappropriate behaviour goes is anyone's guess. We've shown his image to known prostitutes but without anyone giving a positive ID. The Coroner won't be releasing the body as yet and Mrs Kumar is acceptant of that. I'll keep a watching brief over the poor woman." April smiled.

Cyril placed his hand on her arm. "Thanks. Good point regarding the chameleon."

Chapter Twenty-Nine

Mrs Rhodes's flat was, at first glance, just as Cyril had expected. It was situated on the ground floor and at the rear, the north-facing side of a rather poorly maintained Victorian, stone-built semi. In its day it would have been a majestic building with a coach house to the rear and relatively large gardens. Considering the general state of disrepair to the structure, the garden contradicted the overall appearance as it was extremely well kept.

"Someone takes care of that area better than the house." He pointed to the garden.

A rusting, metal fire escape, a later addition, which seemed to criss-cross the gable end, did not enhance the overall aesthetics of the architecture. It quickly became obvious that the house was made up of three floors of apartments. Cyril looked at the splash of daubed paint. The runs from each letter flowed down the wall in varying lengths and thicknesses. It clearly stated that Flats 1A, 2A, 3A were situated in the direction of the arrow pointing to the back of the property. Cyril made his way under the fire escape and into the rear yard. He found the door to the flats. Rubbish overflowed from one of the refuse bins that lined a far wall. Again they were marked with the same pink paint. If he had a pound for every time his feet stuck to carpets, he would be a wealthy man. The prospect of entering Rhodes's flat did not fill him with enthusiasm.

"If the property ever needed an enema I think we found the place they'd administer it," he mumbled to himself as he contemplated what was to come.

***

159

John Barlow sat in Interview Room Four alone apart from the table and three chairs. A camera gave Owen and April a clear view. These preliminary moments when suspects sat alone with their thoughts, and on occasion their guilt were invaluable and helped convey what might never be seen or heard in the interview situation.

He sat twiddling his thumbs, the only evident sign of nervous discomfort exhibited, whilst he stared at the wall. He yawned and then checked his watch before picking up the polystyrene cup from the table. He looked in but it was as he thought, empty. He had drained it ten minutes previously. The time seemed to drag. They had left the door open to give the impression that he was there to help even though Owen had cautioned him. There was also the reassurance that it was procedure and nothing to be concerned about; he was free to walk out at any time. He checked his watch again and stood.

"He doesn't look too concerned. He's getting bored. We'll take him in another brew. Come on."

The light within the room dimmed as Owen and April came through the door and it brought a smile, more out of relief.

"Beginning to think you'd forgotten I was here. Just about to come and look for you."

"Brought you another brew, Mr Barlow. One sugar and not a lot of milk the officer told me. Sorry to keep you. If it's not one thing it's another."

Owen put the drinks on the table and removed the file that had been tucked under his arm.

"Thanks for coming in, your co-operation's greatly appreciated." He allowed time for Barlow to settle again before starting his questioning. "Tell us a little about your past. What we want to do today is clear you from our enquiries and then you can get back to Clipton."

"How far back do you want me to go?"

"A brief history and then we'll ask if we need more clarification on certain points." He tapped the file with his index finger, smiled and sipped some tea. "I have to say that this is being recorded, again it's procedure that ensures your rights."

"Don't I need a lawyer or something?"

"If you wish but as I explained you're free to go whenever you choose. You've not been arrested; you're here offering honest help in the ongoing enquiries. After all, when was the last time you had a death at your place of work?"

"Afghanistan. I saw a number of deaths not to mention those maimed. To answer your question… Lost count of the deaths at the last place of work and in my present employment at least fifteen." He paused and counted on his hands as he thought of the names. "Yes, I've buried fifteen."

Owen realised he had asked the wrong question and could have kicked himself.

"Look, Sergeant, let's get this over with."

John Barlow went through his life methodically; most of it matched what they had on file. The troubles he had experienced after leaving the forces could be attributed to his inability to settle. He described his frontline experiences and a passion for alcohol and women.

"It was Ian who handed me the lifeline. I drifted into a hostel in Ripon of all places. I was once in barracks near the city and I had happy memories of the place what with the Hornblower and the traditions. I thought that returning to a place that had only happy memories for me might help get my life back on an even keel. I was desperate to regain some sort of stability. I went along to a help group run by the church and it was there that I met Ian. He wasn't running it but when I talked through my history, and my time in the army, it must have struck a nerve. Afterwards he came over and asked about my military life. He was a Marine, I believe. It was then that he offered me the post on a month's trial. What I liked was that he didn't ask for any assurances, he trusted me. If he'd said you have to do this and that I'd have told him to fuck off…" April turned and looked at him and then at Owen. "… Excuse me, sorry! That was about two years ago. I owe him a lot."

161

***

Cyril pressed the bell labelled Flat 1A and waited. He caught a glimpse of the net curtain moving in the downstairs window; it lodged, leaving a narrow gap. Theresa Rhodes came to the door. She was more attractive than he had envisaged. The photograph they had on file must have been taken on a bad day! He was expecting an overweight female still in pyjamas looking rather the worse for wear and still holding a can.

"Mrs Rhodes?"

She smiled. "Police? I've been expecting a visit."

"I'm DCI Bennett and this is DC Mistra. May we come in?"

For the second time in a few minutes, Cyril was amazed. He had really expected to walk into a tip; empty bottles, left over takeaway packages, a room in total disarray, but he stood in a lounge area that was immaculate. It was clear that the furnishings were probably donated but they were ordered and clean.

"I'm sorry for your loss, Mrs Rhodes, it must have come as a dreadful shock."

There was a pause as she glanced at a framed photograph on the wall of a very young child; he assumed it to be a pre-school picture of Angela.

"She trod a fine line. She'd threatened suicide on occasions but that was usually when she couldn't get her own way. Never thought she'd do it. She always blamed the voices!"

Cyril gave her a few moments to reflect. She kissed her finger and placed it on the child in the photograph.

"I'm sorry but we'll need you to identify formally that the body of the young lady we hold is that of your daughter. Would you be in a position to do that or is there a relative who might help?"

"No, that's my job. I've not been the best of mothers but I've never run away from my responsibilities. Whenever it suits."

Shakti gave a smile before looking back at Cyril. She noted how he was very compassionate in situations like this allowing people to feel supported. She was learning.

"It probably reflects badly but I've tried over the last two years to get things turned around. I've had a good deal of support, as you can see from the flat, and I'm grateful. You wouldn't think it looking at me now but I did well at school, Detective Chief Inspector. I achieved three good 'A' levels and went to college but fell in with a bad crowd. I had a very strict upbringing, allowing very little freedom and when I arrived at college it was just the opposite of what I'd been used to. I saw a different life and I embraced it fully. However, I found the wrong people. I became a bit of a wild child.

"It wasn't long before I dropped out, pregnant at nineteen with no prospects. I couldn't go home, not to meet my parents' displeasure. Baby, drugs, sleeping rough, prostitution all followed. When they took Angie away I was still an addict. Tomorrow was always going to be the day I'd say no to drugs… Tomorrow never comes when you're dependent. I could cope with her when she was little but then it got worse. I earned money the wrong way and she was taken from me. I was an unsuitable mother! The child was in danger. However, she kept running away and like a pigeon always found me, even when I changed accommodation. It was then that the penny dropped and I realised I had to be a better parent."

"Her father?" Shakti asked, warming to Theresa as both a woman and a mother.

"We didn't stay together long. Tried to pimp me all the time and I was frightened for Angie. I was right too to leave considering all you hear about the grooming gangs and the like. Some men want them young and I was damned sure it wasn't going to happen to my little girl. As you police know from your records she didn't receive the best of parenting or schooling. She was more than a little wild. Jesus, when she came home one day and I saw the teardrop tattoo on her face I went ballistic. Without that and the studs she would be such an attractive girl."

It was only then did Theresa start to break down. Her breathing changed, her shoulders began to heave and the tears began to flow. "It's my fault all this. If I'd got myself together sooner, been more of a mother, she might still be playing that bloody awful music that makes everything shake."

That memory helped her to gain a little more control as a smile came to her lips. "The neighbours didn't appreciate it either; we had a number of complaints from Mr Hill, whose bedroom backs on to Angie's. He and Angie got on well until she played her music in the night. He used to bang on the wall whenever he was in. However, by the next day they'd be friends again. He does a wonderful job on the garden."

Shakti jotted down the name.

"May we see your daughter's room, Mrs Rhodes? We'll be sensitive but you realise…"

"Touch what you need. I'm not a sentimental person. What's gone's gone. Sad I know, but keeping her room as it was when she left it last will not bring her back."

Cyril smiled and he and Shakti were directed to the room.

***

"Do you attend any of the church services, Mr Barlow?" April asked.

"If you'd seen what I'd seen you wouldn't believe there's a God. When you see innocents killed in the name of religion how can you? I don't believe Fella did either. Sometimes, especially after reading about children strapped into suicide vests, he'd cry. Being ex-military, we'd often chat about the present campaigns, ISIL dominating much of that. I've seen him physically shake with anger and cry, especially after the Manchester and the London terrorist attacks. I'm sure if it weren't for the community stuff he's involved in he'd have gone, left the church completely."

"Did he say that to you?"

"He mentioned that his work seemed to have little value in today's extreme society with its multicultural and commercially driven dominance over traditional family values. He felt that he had little to offer in defence and that he was stealing a living as fewer and fewer people attended his services. He realised that if he were to combine all his churches into one he wouldn't fill Clipton unless it was Christmas!"

Owen took a deep breath and tapped April's leg beneath the table. "So those were his actual words, *Stealing a living*?"

Owen wrote the number 3 on a piece of paper and pushed it across to April. "Did he say that only to you or was it common knowledge?"

Barlow spread his hands. "How on earth can I answer that? I worked for him and I hope he considered me a friend, but I wasn't his keeper."

Owen nodded. "You mentioned that you have to walk round the church to check that all's well. What time is that usually?"

"I don't have to, it's something I started when people began nicking from churches. I don't have set times. You learned in the forces to vary your patrols so as not to get caught out. I've been known to do four or five checks, particularly if there's been a report of local lead theft. Some buggers will leave nothing alone. What's strange is that I didn't notice the disturbance of the compost bin. You'd have thought that there'd be bits left, particularly if it were done in the dark and that they'd have emptied the lot."

"When's your day off?"

"Wednesday."

Owen checked his file. Fella was found on Tuesday. He sat back. He glanced to see April look in her file before extracting a photograph. He frowned wondering what she had to show him.

165

"Mr Barlow, I'm sorry that this isn't a particularly good photograph but have you ever seen this woman in Clipton, at church or with Reverend Fella?"

Owen leaned forward realising that she had passed over one of the photographs they held of Tracy Phillips. Barlow picked it up and looked at it carefully. He shook his head. He then covered the person's hair with his thumb.

"I've not seen her but I've seen a bloke who could well be her brother, a tall guy. He was talking to the vicar by the pyramid grave a few weeks back. Seen him before that but I can't recall when."

Owen was now nearly leaning over the table. "Do you remember a name?"

"No. I walked past them with a barrow. He had a woollen hat on and his collar turned up. If I remember they seemed to be having a heated discussion about the grave. Just the body language, I don't know, but they were all smiles when I went past. As soon as they thought I was out of earshot they started again."

Chapter Thirty

Cyril stood and looked around Angie's room. It took a while for the bizarre sight to sink in. The right side of the room appeared as if a bomb had exploded. Clothes and magazines were spread haphazardly across the floor yet the left side was orderly and neat; it was as if there were two rooms in one. His attention focussed on the myriad posters decorating the walls. At first glance many of the posters to the right of the bed appeared innocent, mostly pop group images but on closer inspection they were all linked in some ways to the occult. To the right above the untidy bed was a rough, felt tip pen drawing of a Pentacle. Cyril pointed.

"That's a pentagram, sign of witchcraft. Originally a Christian symbol showing the five wounds of Christ."

Shakti moved closer to examine the posters. One to the right almost filled the space and depicted a mass of shadowy figures with large lettering proclaiming *The Church of Satan* and the date 6/6/6. Others warned that the signs of Satan were all around you. She turned catching a glimpse of a poster of the girl band Little Mix.

"That's better, a girl band poster. I had this type of thing on my wa..." Shakti's voice faded away when she saw the title, *Black Magic*. "Who's put all this shit into her head? There's Katy Perry too, *Satanic Ritual*. I wonder if this is where Angie goes when she's high on glue or gas?"

The posters to the left side of the room were of singers, horses and flowers. There was even a cross, again roughly drawn, to the left as if in direct conflict and therefore dynamically opposing the pentagram.

"It's like the room belongs to two people," Shakti observed. "Good me, bad me."

167

"Or two conflicting personalities," Cyril said as he left. He had touched nothing.

"Mrs Rhodes, I want a Forensic team to go through your daughter's room. How long has she been fascinated by the occult?"

"It's the voices. She told me that she separates and traps them in her room where she feels they're secure and where she can leave them, the good voice and the evil one. She's always believed that nobody likes her because of me, she says no one likes the daughter of a junkie and a harlot. She'd tell me that in one breath and then in the next she'd tell me she loved me. She'd cling to me as if I were about to leave for ever."

"What did she call you?"

"A junkie and a harlot amongst other things!"

Cyril looked at Shakti and registered that she had also picked up on the word. "I wonder why she used the word *harlot*, seems rather a bizarre term for a youth of today."

"Probably street talk, Inspector. If that was all she called me, then I could live with that."

"Did you seek professional help for Angie, Mrs Rhodes?" Shakti asked, aware that Angie had seen psychiatrists in the past.

"She'd go once or twice and then if she knew she had an appointment I wouldn't find her for a day or two. These professionals..." She emphasised the word *professional*. "... don't take kindly to missed appointments even when they're dealing with the mentally ill. The only person she seemed to get on well with was Mr Hill, the gardener, even though she drove him daft with her music. He's a sensitive man, keeps himself to himself."

"We'll pop and see him," Cyril said as he stood to leave.

"Unless you're prepared to go to Southport you won't find him. Supposedly goes every year to some convention. Angie did tell me but then..."

"Do you know his full name?"

168

She shook her head. "Sid, Simon or Sam. We always call him Mr Hill."

"The Police Liaison Officer will be in touch," Cyril said as he held out his hand.

"She came this morning. Asian girl." She inadvertently looked at Shakti. "She's arranged to be with me when I see Angie later."

Chapter Thirty-One

On their return, Cyril caught a glimpse of John Barlow leaning against a car outside the police station. He was staring at the building eagerly exhaling the smoke from his nostrils. The tobacco smell hung near the entrance doors where he had initially lit the cigarette, a languid reminder to Cyril of one of his less attractive habits. He and Shakti moved to the front counter, signed in and flipped the lanyards over their heads. Owen and April approached them. Owen held up the photograph of Tracy Philips.

"Did you see Barlow leaving? Seems our Tracy has a brother or if not, there's a bloke seen talking to Ian Fella who has a striking resemblance. It appeared, according to Barlow, that he and Fella were having a heated discussion but he couldn't say what about. And where was that taking place do you think, sir?"

Cyril hated twenty questions and let Owen know. "I've no time for games, Owen, just tell me the facts."

"The pyramid grave."

Cyril said nothing. He looked at both April and Owen. "And Barlow? Is he telling the truth or just making up a story?"

"Only time and evidence will tell us that, sir. You said we have to keep an open mind."

Cyril just looked back at Owen. "So why show him the picture of Phillips at this stage in the investigation?"

Owen thought for a moment. "With the label containing her name being found there, I just thought it was worth the ask. Maybe she went to the church after she disappeared." Owen did well thinking on the spur of the moment, after all, he was the senior officer interviewing Barlow.

"To keep an open mind, Owen, right! You do know that it also gives him the opportunity to send us on a complete and utter wild bloody goose chase. This investigation is already under budget scrutiny. There's pressure to get results and we can't afford to go around North Yorkshire looking for some guy who is or might be a figment of Barlow's imagination or guilt. They want a murderer apprehended, maybe as they've said, a potential serial killer. Right now, for purely financial reasons, they're not too concerned about a woman who went missing eighteen months ago and quite frankly neither am I."

Owen looked at April and then back at Cyril. He pulled a face suggesting it might be wise to keep counsel for the moment but Cyril had other ideas.

"Who had the bright idea to show the photograph in the first place?"

Owen immediately claimed responsibility. "Sorry, as I said, I just thought..."

"Spur of the moment or planned?" Cyril's retort was rhetorical. "You know what thought did, Owen, don't you? Thought followed a muck cart thinking it was a wedding. All of you, the Incident Room now! We need a perspective on this and on the observations we've just made from our visit to the Rhodes's flat."

Owen tapped April on the back and put his finger to his lips before whispering in her ear. "His bark's worse than his bite." He winked at her and smiled. "He'll be fine in ten minutes, you watch."

***

Felicity walked up the path and saw Graham. The dappled shadows flickered across him. His book was next to him on the bench, otherwise he was alone. He simply stared ahead oblivious of her approach. There was no movement.

"Dad?" she called from a short distance away and he turned. "Are you all right?" She could tell from his facial

171

expression that he was far from the man she had left earlier in the day. "It looks as though you've lost a tanner and found a penny!" She laughed, hoping to lighten the mood.

"I suppose you could say that's true. What time is it?"

"Just coming up to twelve." She put his book in her bag before handing him his sticks. "Come on, I'll buy you lunch at Betty's, the queue isn't bad but I've been the perfect daughter-in-law and pre-booked, I know you hate to stand outside and wait." She watched for a change of expression but none came.

Chapter Thirty-Two

April brought a tray of drinks into the Incident Room.

"Sorry for the strong words earlier," Cyril smiled as he looked at each member of his team before removing the cup and saucer from the tray. "Coincidences seem to be plaguing me at the moment, what with that and the disturbing experience of seeing that room this morning. On reflection, April, I think showing the photograph was the correct action."

Owen turned to April and raised an eyebrow. Cyril had known all along that it had been her initiative. Owen would not have been so naïve.

Cyril then glanced at Owen and smiled. "I'd have done the same, Owen. Well done. It's good to see that you think about others first. This team we have here is very important to me. Well done!" He paused and then asked Shakti to outline their visit.

"Angie Rhodes, from what we've witnessed today, was one mixed-up young lady. The only friend she had, according to her mum, was some guy who had the front flat in their block. She drove him daft playing her loud music at all times of the day and night but they were still very friendly."

"Sexually friendly?" Owen asked leaning over to pick up the only wrapped biscuit on the plate.

Cyril frowned.

"Well, an old guy might tolerate a good deal of disturbance if she were cooperative in certain ways. Is that where she got her money? Or is it a case of like mother like daughter?"

"We only have rumours that they may have been on the game, neighbourly gossip. Mother's a complete contradiction. You have a certain expectation when you're about to meet a

173

long-term, registered drug abuser but she was remarkably in control of her world, articulate too. However, from our discussion, she had no control over her daughter other than the bond of love and the fact that they shared the same flat. The daughter always demonstrated that she wanted to be with her mother, even in the darker times."

"What about this neighbour?"

"We couldn't speak with him as he's away…" Shakti looked at Cyril.

"Southport she said."

"Southport on some conference or convention. Shakti check his details for that address. His name's Hill, a Simon or a Sid. Check also current conventions in Southport, there can't be many."

Shakti made a call requesting the information.

Cyril noticed that April was flicking through her notes.

"Wouldn't be a Samuel would it, sir?" April suddenly put down her mug of coffee and looked at Cyril.

He said nothing feeling rather put on the spot. "Why?"

"May I just use the computer?" She was already on her feet crossing to the nearest machine. She tapped in her password, her fingers flying across the keyboard and then she read the details on the screen as Cyril stood and moved behind her.

"There, sir, as I thought. Samuel Hill was one of the founding members of the Gideon Society back in 1899, 1 July, 1899 to be exact, along with a John Nicholson and William Knights. It might be just a coincidence."

"Coincidences!" Cyril said out loud as he immediately thought again of the letter he had received and the questions that he had wrestled with for so long. A historical coincidence… that was one of the reasons he had wanted to be a copper in the first place. His life now seemed to be full of coincidences and he was determined to separate the facts from the fiction. It was like when you buy a red car, every car you seem to then see is red!

"Is Mr Hill our Gideon Fletcher?" April asked.

That was a bloody good question and Cyril had been thinking the very same thing. "We need to find our Mr Hill or we need a warrant to search his premises but we won't get one on a pure coincidence."

Shakti's phone rang. She listened before slipping her hand over the phone as she relayed the information. "There's a Christian convention, a seventy-two-hour prayer meeting going on in Southport at the moment."

"Shakti, ask them to get a list of those attending in any capacity and see if there's anyone by the name of Fletcher, Hill, Nicholson or Knights."

Cyril nodded. "Good, April, very good. So what else?"

"It was something that Barlow said. The cross was found at the vicarage containing the number three, which we now believe is a reference to theft. Barlow said that Fella was concerned that he was and I quote, *stealing a living, as he didn't seem able to build a stronger congregation*; the congregation in fact was diminishing and no matter what he tried, he couldn't seem to entice more people to the services. Fella said on more than one occasion that if it weren't for the community element to his job, he'd have left, given up his calling and the church."

"He said that to Barlow?"

Owen nodded.

"I wonder if he said that to Gideon Fletcher on the night they met? Remind me, was there a bag of hair attached to Fella's cross?"

"As with the others, dyed scarlet. It only contained Fella's hair."

Chapter Thirty-Three

Graham Baker sat opposite his daughter-in-law. He ate very little of the Swiss onion quiche that he usually ordered but he was on his second glass of Gewurztraminer. Felicity watched as his hand shook slightly.

"Are you alright?" she asked. "You don't seem yourself. Usually you're bubbling after your morning in the fresh air telling me all about your observations."

He looked straight at her and lied. "I'm fine. Sometimes the discomfort in my back is more severe than usual. Let's leave it there." He took what appeared to be a short blister pack from his shirt breast pocket, and popped out two tablets. They were his last two and from his earlier conversation with Sam, they would be the last he would receive. He put one back into his pocket and swallowed the other, finishing the white wine in one go. Felicity was surprised to see him then attract the waitress's attention before pointing to his glass.

"Have you seen the doctor for stronger tablets?"

"He says that I can't have the ones that help because there's a chance of addiction. Bloody hell, if they had the constant pain I have, they'd take them believe me. They just don't listen! It's all about bloody budgets and looking after all these people coming into the country. Those who've paid in all their lives are soon forgotten. In fact the sooner you die the better, then they're not paying out on pensions." His voice grew in volume above the respectful murmur of the dining room. A number of diners looked across disapprovingly at their table, as did the maître d'.

"You're embarrassing me, Dad. Please keep your voice down and try to enjoy your lunch."

Graham turned to observe the number of staring faces and sighed. He looked back at her anxious face. It was then that she saw a tear roll down his cheek as he mouthed the word, *sorry*. She slipped her hand across the table and patted his.

"Never mind, it's nothing." Felicity smiled and handed him her napkin. "I understand."

He shook his head. "I don't think you do and I doubt you ever will." He forced a smile to his lips. "I'm sorry, I've been a fool!"

"Don't worry, everyone is eating, it's forgotten."

"You really don't understand."

***

Felicity parked outside the bungalow. She normally dropped him off and left but today she felt as though he needed her there. She helped him from the car and they went inside. Graham's wife, Pat, sensing something was wrong, came out of the kitchen to meet them. Felicity smiled. "He's not been too good, a lot of discomfort with his back."

Pat helped him to his chair and brought up a footstool. "He can have an afternoon nap then he should be fine."

They moved to the lounge door. Felicity noticed his shaking hand travel to his breast pocket and retrieve what she believed to be a tablet. He popped it into his mouth and put his head back as if relieved to have managed to swallow it. He slipped back the empty foil and plastic wrapping.

"What tablets does he keep taking?" Felicity asked Pat. "He seems to take a lot more than I remember."

"For the pain I think, my dear. If he doesn't take them he gets extremely annoyed over the smallest of things. Says he can't sleep and goes out in the car quite early for a paper. Sometimes he seems to go out at a ridiculously early hour. Mind you, I'm one to talk, I'm the opposite, can't seem to get up in a morning. Graham thinks it's all the fresh air from gardening. More like old age and poverty!" She chuckled. "Thanks for taking

177

him out. Cleaning's done and most of the ironing. Glad to get him from under my feet. I keep telling him he's turning into a real grumpy old man!"

Felicity bent and kissed her cheek. "Love you. Please keep an eye on him, I know he's not himself."

Graham heard the front door close as he considered his next move.

***

April's phone rang and she answered. "Thanks. Send it over ASAP. Thanks again." She turned to see the three faces looking in anticipation in her direction. "None of those names is on the list. They're sending it over along with contact details or email addresses of those present. Some information they don't have as they were walk in."

"Then it's got to be a warrant," Cyril said as he collected the papers. "I need to speak to Mada. You all need to eat soon seeing as Owen has cleared the majority of the biscuits."

***

The anxiety conveyed in Felicity's phone call to her husband was enough to bring him home from work early. He promised, traffic permitting, that he would be home by three; he arrived fifteen minutes early and within the hour they were at his parents' house.

Rupert looked at Felicity. "Are you sure before we do this? You know what Dad's like!"

"You'll have to trust my female intuition. Something is seriously not right."

As they approached the front door, it became clear that his father was far from well. Even from the outside they could hear his ranting. Felicity took her emergency key from her bag and opened the front door. Suddenly the anger seemed to

178

enwrap them in the hallway as Graham's voice boomed from the lounge.

"No one understands, not even you. All you do is bloody sleep when I'm pacing in agony. Look at you sitting there in floods of tears, you're no bloody good, never have been since my accident. I should never have listened to you. It's your fault all this. Claim for the accident, you said, *exaggerate your disability and they'll compensate us more*, compensate us for what? Go on, tell me what happiness your scheme's brought us?"

Hearing the front door close he walked to the window, his sticks still resting on the chair. Rupert rushed into the lounge his eyes immediately alighting on his mother. She was sitting huddled on the settee, her apron drawn up to mask her face as she wept openly. His father stood, red faced and simply stared, his fists clenched tightly to his side showing a marked tremor.

Rupert sat next to his mother, wrapped a protective arm around her shoulders and kissed her forehead. "Come on, Felicity's in the kitchen. She'll make you some tea. We could all do with some tea. I need to talk to Dad."

Graham was just about to speak.

"You say nothing do you hear me, nothing!" Rupert did not raise his voice but it quickly became evident that he would not tolerate his father's anger. "From what I've heard and from what I can see, you've ranted enough. Sit down, now!"

He gently brought his mother to her feet and led her into the kitchen. Graham stood defiantly, he was not going to tolerate his son dictating to him, not in his own home.

"I told you to sit! If you're in as much pain as you seem to be announcing to the neighbourhood, you'd be holding on to those sticks or you'd be resting. Now sit."

Graham reluctantly moved to his chair.

"What's going on? Felicity's seen a change in you over the weeks, from before you found that paper. Suddenly we have today's shocking behaviour whilst you were out and now at home. What scheme were you screaming about?"

His father looked down at his feet.

***

Felicity sat opposite Pat. She was still upset, and every now and again she blew her nose into her handkerchief. "My tiredness, his early mornings, his pain, the tablets, I don't know. Maybe we've both changed, maybe its old age."

"What's he taking?"

"Paracetamol, that's all the doctor will give him. According to them he shouldn't be in pain after the operation he had. There's no evidence of nerve damage; he's had three scans. He seems to just want painkillers."

"And what are you taking?"

"Me?" she laughed. "Too much wine maybe but I don't take medicine. You know I believe that we all consume too many chemicals. Let nature take its true course, that's always been my motto."

"Where does he keep his tablets?"

"Since the accident we have separate rooms as you know. In his drawer I would think." Felicity stood. "Flis, you can't go in there! He'll know you've been in."

She ignored the comment, mainly because she could detect a false degree of anxiety as if her mother-in-law were hoping that she would. She pushed open the door. The curtains were drawn. Opening them enabled the light to flood in. The room was ordered and precise. She noticed that the drawers were not all fully closed but were each open to a different extent. She only touched the bottom, bedside drawer and withdrew it completely. Ignoring the drawer, she ran her hand along the bottom of the frame and was immediately rewarded. She held four small blister packs in her hand. Turning one over, she read the print, *Amitriptyline*. She removed her phone and searched on line before reading the information. She noted that the side effects matched many of Pat's symptoms. She ran her hand round again but there was nothing else. Sliding the drawer back, she returned to the kitchen.

***

"Felicity tells me that you've been taking more tablets than usual. What tablets are those?"

Graham was silent. His hands shook when he lifted them from the chair arm and Rupert noticed the beads of sweat forming under his arms darkening his light-coloured shirt.

"She mentioned the tablets you had today. What's in your shirt pocket, Dad?"

A hand immediately went to the pocket but Rupert was too quick, having already anticipated his father's move. He pushed his hand away, thrust two fingers into the pocket and withdrew the part of the empty blister pack that had held the two tablets. His father tried to grab it but it was now secured in Rupert's hand.

"A lot of fuss over paracetamol, Dad. What are they?" He moved away looking at the print on the damaged foil that had covered the two empty spaces. The word Xanax, 3mg, was clearly written twice alongside the dosage.

Felicity came into the room and passed the packs she had found to Rupert. "Hidden beneath his drawer. Strangely, I used to hide love letters in exactly the same place when I was a teen to stop my brother from finding and reading them."

"How dare you go into my room and rummage!"

Rupert lifted a finger in front of his father's face. "If you utter one more word I'll strip that room."

Felicity studied Graham who now not only seemed shocked but looked a defeated and tired old man.

"Did you take these as well, Dad?" Her caring voice seemed to calm him and offer a way back.

Graham shook his head. "I'm so sorry. It's the pain. Nobody understands, nobody apart from Sam. Thank God he knew what I was going through."

181

"Who's Sam?"

"I don't really know other than I met him when I was by The Stray. He was sitting on my favourite bench. I remember his first words to me, after noticing my sticks. He'd been in the army and some injury he'd sustained caused him a great deal of distress. He recommended those." He pointed to the pack Rupert held. "Said they worked wonders. I met him again and he gave me two packs, ten in each pack. He said to take them three times a day, that they were the best things for pain relief. Spot on he was. I tried to get them from my GP but he refused me saying that the side effects were severe and that there was a risk of becoming immune to their efficacy and a strong possibility of dependency. This is from a man who doesn't believe that I'm in any sort of pain. The man's delusional, a fool and an idiot and I told him so."

Rupert looked at Felicity and shook his head. "So where have these two come from that you took today?"

Graham fidgeted nervously. He held his hands tightly to keep them from shaking. "I've told you, Sam gets them if I do some morning errands now and again."

"What errands?"

Leaving them, Felicity returned to Pat. She also had questions she needed answering.

Chapter Thirty-Four

Cyril crossed The Stray. He looked at the familiar sight of The Coach and Horses. The metal penny-farthing hanging from the end of the building always made him smile. He had quickly grown to enjoy the pub's hospitality. It did not allow children or dogs and there was no TV, music or games machines, just a perfect pint that varied from week to week and if you wanted it, polite conversation. It was a place where he could be left alone to become lost in his thoughts after difficult days. Of course if they served Black Sheep, then it would have to be that, after all it was his preferred poison but he had learned that there were so many excellent local breweries and the chance of finding another favourite made for a welcome change.

He sat in a corner. He needed to reflect on the day. Interestingly, Mada had also been surprised by Mrs Rhodes's stoical attitude. She had identified her daughter with a degree of control that Mada had rarely witnessed; there was clearly sadness but also respect. The way that she had touched the body, clearly showed a mother's tenderness as had the brief outpouring of grief. It was clear that the Family Liaison Officer had time and respect for her.

Cyril reflected on the words that Mada had reported that the mother had said on arriving back at her flat. *Although I've never really been a good mother and there have been times when Angie wasn't with me, I realise that she was always with me, even when she was in care. Now, of course, she's dead, no longer the homing bird she always was. Suddenly and selfishly, I feel as though I'm in a dark void, where there's little reason to seek the light, to go on and be better.* She clearly realised that she had missed so many opportunities to be a good mother and now it was too late.

183

Cradling another pint, his mind crashed agonisingly to his own position, a situation not too dissimilar from that of the bereaved mother. He took the envelope and reread the contents. How many times had he read it? He could not be sure. Should his stubborn arrogance prevent him from making peace with his father? If he went would it be for purely selfish reasons or was he prepared to forgive and forget? Like the voices Angie Rhodes heard so clearly, he was now experiencing a similar dilemma.

His mind suddenly turned to the family from Ripon; the abuse the daughter had suffered at the hands of her parents made him shudder. He remembered how dignified she had been when she discovered the truth behind her past. It should not have come as a surprise but he realised that not everyone has a perfect upbringing, a childhood filled with wonder and happy memories. The years tumbled in his mind and although he could see the sadness, he could also remember the joy. At least he had enjoyed the security that brought with it an education and a freedom of choice.

The landlord looked across at Cyril and could clearly see that he was wrestling mentally with an issue; he had grown to appreciate when to chat and when to leave well alone. Misguidedly he presumed it to be a police issue but thankfully left him in peace.

Cyril opened his notebook to a clean page. It was unmarked white. Smoothing it with his hand, he took his pen, adding a small spot of ink. He drained his glass, picked up the notebook and approached the bar.

"Another, Cyril?" The landlord smiled as he collected a fresh glass in anticipation.

"No, Ken, thank you. What do you notice here?"

He pushed the notebook across the bar. Ken picked it up and studied the page.

"Trick question? You coppers are all the same. A black spot, there." He pointed to the small dot.

"Correct, Ken. Tell me, didn't you see a whole page of white too?"

He pulled a face. "Took that for granted, Cyril, thought that was too obvious."

Both smiled. "Maybe we just don't look too carefully at what's around us." Cyril leaned over, shook Ken's hand and turned to leave.

Once outside, Cyril took out his phone and tapped in the familiar number. He stared across at the now dark sky streaked with fine, deep, red lines. He checked his watch before shaking his wrist and looking again. Julie was quick to answer.

"Julie, I've made up my mind. I'm going to see him one last time. I'll not be attending the funeral, but I want to see him, I want to forgive and forget. I also want to see his wife, Wendy, my stepmother. Will you come?"

"In all the time we've been together you'd never talked about your past and in some ways that's fine, that's private. I shall be honoured to go with you."

"Saturday, we'll leave early. Pack an overnight bag just in case we need to stay. And Julie..." he paused.

"Cyril?"

"I love you!" He hung up before she could reply. For the first time since receiving the letter, he suddenly felt so much easier, a weight had lifted from his shoulders. Turning, he slipped down the passageway and as he walked down Robert Street his hand touched the envelope that he now kept permanently with him. It was the only link he had to his youth. He was determined from now on to always search for the white paper and not the odd black spot. He removed his phone again and dialled Julie for the second time.

"I love you too," she said before he could speak. "Leaving a girl after such sweet talk is not acceptable." She giggled.

"I was heading home but I need to eat and have a chat. Fancy Italian? L'Albero Delle Noci?"

"I'll be there in twenty minutes, you know what to order for me."

***

Cyril waited. The room was small and busy but he had been shown to a quiet table. He had placed his order while Marco fretted about when Miss Julie would arrive. Checking his watch, Cyril reassured him that she would be there at any moment and as if by magic, she entered the restaurant. Marco made an immediate move with all his flamboyance and kissed her, mumbling a string of compliments in Italian before bringing her to Cyril's table.

He kissed her. "Can't compete with the suave Italian devil I'm afraid."

"So, you've decided." She sipped her wine as the meal was brought to them.

"Risotto, always risotto!" Marco turned breaking into song.

***

The hair dye, the mesh trays and the gloves were put into a small box before the lid was taped shut. Tonight it would be dumped in a litterbin, one of many that were spread around The Stray. Night, under the security of the dark, was the only feasible time to move. The daylight hours were a time for resting and planning for the final act of correction. Besides, the cellar offered little differentiation between night and day. The temperatures seemed to remain relatively constant and the natural light was marginal during the day. Having the only key ensured security and so the lights were left on constantly; it had become the norm and now nobody took any notice, after all they were not paying for the wasted electricity, the landlord was.

There was one small cross left on the shelf to which the fishing line and bag were already attached. There was no number, a deliberate omission. However, there was a large cross, made from rough lengths of timber. The cross-lap cuts had been carefully fashioned in both pieces. Strong adhesive was squeezed from the tube trapped within the mastic gun until a stream of grey snakes covered the timber. With care this was offered to a vertical chalk line that had been marked on the wall and as much force as possible applied. Within half an hour a strong enough bond would have formed to allow the same procedure to be done to the patibulum. This would be offered to the cross-lap cut made in the vertical and the crucifixion cross would be assembled. The work was now near enough complete. Once the cross was fixed and the glue set there was nothing more that could be done. Hill moved towards the cupboard, removed a tin of rice pudding, snapped back the ring-pull on the top before eating the contents cold and directly from the can. He stared at the hammer and the horseshoe nails that sat on the workbench.

All was nearly ready. There was no time to rest. It would not take them long to discover that he had disappeared. On his last nocturnal trip he had seen the local paper and read that they had found the girl's body. He had heard the many feet in the girl's flat above him as he had worked in the cellar. He had one more visit to the pyramid, one more instruction of correction and his job would be done. God had called and he would be relieved to be free. All of this, all of his past would be crossed out, wiped clean. He would be reborn. Collecting a number of photographs, he nailed them to the cross, a history… his story… her story; the horseshoe nails' sharp tips drove well into the timber. The hammer and the remaining nails were wrapped in an old towel and slid into the shoulder bag.

From the shelf he took a bottle containing Nitric acid. From the drawer he then brought out a Jif lemon; the inside had been lined with a thin layer of bees' wax as an additional, secure coating. Acid will not eat through wax. Slowly using a thin funnel the plastic, yellow lemon was filled to about two-thirds. It was the only weapon he would carry, the only deterrent should things not go according to plan. The bottle was returned to the shelf and the Jif container secreted in the shoulder bag.

He stripped before moving to the sink. Picking up the shaving foam and a razor, within five minutes the stubble on his head had disappeared. The arms, the legs, the pubic bone, the eyebrows were all shaved. He towel-dried his skin, dabbing at the more tender areas of naked flesh before standing in front of the mirror. Mr Hill indeed! A laugh broke from the parted lips as he whispered, *Welcome back, Tracy. I've missed you.* She then quoted the message that she had given to Baker to hand to the police. *I've not gone anywhere. I've just stopped walking these streets, a shadow of my former self... maybe... you just don't see... do you?*

Tracy Phillips stood in front of the mirror, her breasts exposed, her body totally shaved of hair. She slipped on the woollen tunic, tied the rope belt loosely around her waist and knelt before the cross.

"I hear you. The time is close. I shall be with you soon, Gideon, very soon."

She stood and walked to the cross and placed her lips on the centre of the patibulum. "This is how the harlot will rest." She took a long, last look at the photographs.

Turning, she removed the gown stuffing it into a tote bag before dressing in jeans, a thick shirt and a hooded top. She slipped out into the darkness. A hand flicked the switch to put the cellar in darkness for the first time that she could remember. She had no idea why but she just felt as though she were being guided on the final path of her journey. She adjusted both shoulder bags ready for what was her last journey as Gideon, her final correction. The anticipation of standing by the pyramid grave filled her with a frisson of excitement.

***

"So, you're not a Yorkshireman after all!"

"No, but I've spent more of my life here in Harrogate than any other part of the country and have adapted and adopted many of the traits your men hold so dear. When was the last time you saw my wallet? Have you brought your purse? See, I'm a fast learner." Cyril felt the urge to reveal to her some of his past.

"Nantwich, Cheshire. It was a beautiful market town surrounded by wonderful countryside but close enough to Liverpool and Manchester. Like Harrogate, it was a town known for its salt spas." He paused and Julie could see him drift off as if the spools of an old projector were being rewound, taking him back through the years.

"Everything was perfect up until that day but you know that."

"So why do you want to return to a place that brought you such emotional trauma? You've to have a clear reason, Cyril, and it can't be a decision you take for reasons of selfish guilt. You cannot return to appease your conscience, your trip has to be honest and meaningful."

There was a long pause. Julie deliberately did not reach across for his hand that was extended and flat on the table. She allowed the developing silence to grow and even though it might make Cyril uncomfortable, she felt that this was a critical moment. If he were to waver then she knew that he was not ready to return to his past and she would tell him so. She was aware that he was still emotionally scarred by Liz's death and this could open old wounds.

He looked up and smiled as if he had replayed enough. "There will never be a time when I'll forget and try to accept the true hurt his philandering caused my mother, but I do realise that there always comes a moment to forgive and if ever there was an appropriate one then this is it. After some of the recent events I've seen and experienced in this job of mine, a job that brings me close to families that appear normal from the outside but are nothing but a sham, I have to take stock. This position I hold may have been borne by those early traumas. I feel, on reflection, that I've been lucky to know the strong love and bond of a mother and father. Yes, they may have had a disparate relationship, but I was loved, and in some ways cherished. I have a love of music and art gifted by my mother and a strong work ethic from my father..."

Julie saw his facial expression change and knew what was coming.

"...and a dread of commitment within relationships, a dread of having children of my own for fear of hurting them."

She saw the distant look appear again but then a smile broke across his face. He studied her and she could see the honesty expressed and wondered what he was about to say.

"I might be one hell of a mixed up human being right now but I couldn't be in a happier place. He took her hand and brought it to his lips. "You'd never catch a Yorkshireman do that in public. You've had a narrow escape meeting me, Julie Pritchett, and don't you forget it!"

Marco came over to their table. "I see the risotto was not to your liking, you've left a grain of rice there!" His stubby finger pointed to the offending article. "I'll tell the chef." He winked and cleared away the two bowls. "You two lovebirds need coffees, yes?" he enquired. "Yes, two coffees for two lovebirds."

Chapter Thirty-Five

Rupert and Graham Baker stood at the front desk of Harrogate police station. Neither was in the mood to communicate with the other. Both were angry but each had a different reason for their ire. The duty officer listened carefully as Rupert explained the reason for their visit before he put in a call. Brian Smirthwaite answered.

"Take them to the Reception room, it's less intimidating and I'll be down in five." He turned to his computer and brought up the necessary file on Graham Baker and quickly read it. "Our man who handed in the newspaper." He moved to Shakti's desk and retrieved her file before going to meet them.

Graham sat watched by his son. He was obviously suffering both physically and emotionally.

"After this we'll go to A&E. You need medical help," Rupert said.

Brian Smirthwaite entered and introduced himself. He slipped a Dictaphone on the table between them. "For the record." He smiled. "Now how can we help?"

Rupert explained the situation regarding his father and put the empty blister pack on the table along with the packs of Amitriptyline. "He tells us that these have been given to him by a stranger whom he meets near The Stray close to Montpellier Hill."

Smirthwaite picked them up and read the labels. "One minute." He stood, left and went to the front desk. He handed them to the Desk Sergeant. "Get me the duty doctor and ask him about these. From what I can see, this old guy's going cold turkey."

He returned to the room. "Now, Mr Baker, what's this all about?" He could initially sense a certain reluctance but then he opened up.

"A few years ago I had an accident at work, damaged my spine and I needed three operations. It meant that I couldn't work. My wife had this idea that I should exaggerate the discomfort that it brought me in the hope of receiving greater compensation. Money was a little tight after years of supporting my son through his studies. My wife has never worked. The doctors gave me painkilling injections and then tablets. After a while they told me that they were going to reduce the strength and the dosage to prevent my becoming reliant on the medication. They also said that the pain was more likely psychological. It's all about funding, about budgets not about people and the correct care. All these people flooding into the country going on benefits and receiving immediate health care, that's what they should bloody well stop, not my medication!" He paused. "May I have some water?"

Brian stood, went to the water dispenser and brought back a paper cup.

"Thank you. Where was I?"

"Tablets, Mr Baker. The doctor refused to give you them."

"He'd give me paracetamol and that was it. Anyway, I usually sit on a bench by Montpellier Hill and on this occasion, there was this chap sitting there. I plonked myself down and started reading my book. It can be very warm even in winter, when the sun's out you're protected from the wind. It was then that he addressed me. He said that he'd seen me on a few occasions walking as I do with these two sticks. I told him about my symptoms. He told me that he suffered from acute pain and that he took these tablets that he got from the Internet. Best he'd ever taken for relieving pain, said he was now pain-free. He gave me two packs, twenty tablets and told me to take them three times a day. He was right, within a day I was much better. I could walk without the sticks a bit too."

The duty officer came in and handed Brian a note detailing the tablets.

"So which tablets were these, Mr Baker?"

"Xanax."

Brian nodded. "How long have you been taking 3mg three times a day?"

"For a few weeks, Sam, the man who gave me them said that I might need to up that on occasion. I have to admit that I've doubled the dose. Seem to get the shakes when I don't and get rather cross with the world."

"You mentioned to my duty officer that you did errands for this chap. What kind of errands?"

"I was asked to leave a packet or a rolled-up paper at a set place and at a set time. It was no problem because I wasn't sleeping too well so it was easy for me to be up early. I'd then find a packet left for me at a different location. I sometimes saw the person who was dropping my stuff. A scruffy sod, girl I think although in some light you couldn't be sure. Had a tattoo, here." He pointed to a spot on his face. "Funny I had a feeling that the same person collected what I'd dropped off. If that were the case I can't see why we didn't just use one place."

An alarm bell rang in Brian's head as he immediately thought of Angie Rhodes.

Rupert sat, growing increasingly concerned.

Brian checked his notes. "You handed in a newspaper that you found on a bench. Was this the same bench where you would meet Sam?"

Baker nodded.

"Mr Baker, did Sam give you the paper?"

There was a pause.

"Mr Baker?"

He nodded. "Promised me two extra packs if I handed it in to a copper and said I'd found it on the bench."

"Can you describe Sam?"

Baker was sweating heavily and his hands were shaking.

193

Rupert interjected. "He told me that he had no facial hair, no eyebrows. He said that there was something strange about him but not disconcerting. He always seemed to be smiling, that's what Dad said."

They both looked at Graham who now appeared ashen-faced.

"I've asked a doctor to call. We need to take some blood samples to see just what your father's been given. What about the other tablets?"

"He'd been giving those to Mum. He'd crush them and add them to the wine she enjoyed with her evening meal. Made her sleep. Something Mum never used to do was sleep in in the morning. When we were kids she'd be up at six, winter and summer. This explains why recently she's been in bed till nine!"

"So these were never meant for him?"

"No, he told Sam that it was impossible for him to leave the house early with Mum there and he advised giving her these. I've checked and I believe they've been used in nursing homes as a sedative. Certainly worked with Mum."

Graham suddenly stood. "Think I'm going to be si-"

He leaned forward and vomited. Brian just managed to grab the file and the Dictaphone as the projected liquid spewed across the coffee table.

***

The taxi dropped Tracy Phillips off at Ripon Market Place. She tipped the driver, adjusted the woollen cap, threw the bags over her shoulders, and walked towards the Obelisk where a small crowd had gathered. The Hornblower, standing by one corner, resplendent in his tri-cornered hat and holding what appeared to be a large ox horn decorated with polished copper, was regaling the group of spectators with the history behind the tradition of setting the watch. As he blew the first, long blast, two youths on what appeared to be excuses for motorbikes decided to rev their machines; their low power was compensated with noisy exhausts. It was then that Tracy heard the voice; even above the horn and the wail of the bikes it was clear. Tracy turned. She walked slowly towards them and stood about a metre away. She said nothing. For a moment she stared at them. Neither wore a helmet.

Many in the crowd had turned round as the bikes, leaning on side-stands, were revved but soon returned their attention to the Hornblower who had also ignored the distraction.

"Switch them off, please!" She stared at the larger of the two youths. "I've just been commanded to help you correct your ways. Please you are being weak and selfish, turn them off!"

"Fuck right off! Who the fuck are you to tell us? Commanded my arse." His fist turned the throttle and a banshee-like scream emerged from the exhaust at the same time as Tracy's hand withdrew the plastic Jif lemon from her pocket.

"I've been commanded to tell you that you must stop or your selfish act and sheer foolishness will be corrected. That is the last time." The noise made it impossible for him to hear, he just saw her lips moving and laughed.

"Fuck off you shit. We do what we fucking well want..."

She moved closer and held out her arm as if it were a gun before squeezing the container very hard. A thin, almost invisible stream of nitric acid targeted the youth's laughing eyes. For a moment the laughter remained to be quickly replaced by an uncontrolled, contorted gurn. His hand quickly released the throttle and one engine was quiet as both his hands were brought up to the burning pain that now filled his eyes. Tracy turned to the second youth. "Please, or I shall melt your eyes also."

The noise suddenly stopped apart from the screams from the youth who was now on the floor holding his face. The third long blast from the Hornblower was sufficient to drown out the youth's cries. The other boy went to his friend's aid whilst fumbling with his mobile phone. Tracy moved to the two bikes, removed the keys rendering them silent and walked away. She dropped them into the first available road drain she saw. "If only they'd seen the wisdom in my words. Now one may never see again."

She quickened her step following Kirkgate towards the Cathedral. It would take fifty minutes to walk to Clipton and as the evening was fine she could think of nothing better to do; this would be her last ever visit to the Pyramid. As she crossed the top of Duck Hill she heard the siren. She paused briefly before turning to see the blue flashes from the emergency vehicle illuminate the top of the Obelisk that stood proudly above the darkened rooftops. Either the police or a paramedic was at the scene. She smiled before continuing her walk.

***

Shakti arrived to be met by Brian Smirthwaite. She was dressed for a night out. She slipped on the police lanyard and signed in. "Where is he?"

"Been admitted to hospital, serious case of withdrawal. Baker was addicted to Alprazolam, it's an opioid used as an anti-depressant and a painkiller. They're one of the two most frequently abused prescription drugs in the world so you can imagine the different qualities that'll be available on the net. According to the duty doctor, Baker's a very lucky man. He's not showing any signs of suffering from serious kidney or liver damage; the side effects of this medication, this drug, can be awful. The doctor told me that you can become quickly addicted, in as little as two weeks. They're great for stopping pain only you get used to them and have to take more to achieve the same relief. This Sam had him eating out of his hand. I wonder if he applied the same manipulative strategy to Angie Rhodes? Could she have been the person in the back of Kumar's car or could it have been Sam?"

Smirthwaite regaled her with his chat with Baker.

196

"So the fact that he needed someone to plant the stuff for Angie and also using Angie as a courier, demonstrates that this is Hill, her neighbour, the friendly gardener who would bang on the wall when her music was too loud and be best of mates the next day. He'd be controlling her with whatever he supplied."

"He must have met her initially like he met Baker. Befriended her until she trusted him and then..."

"How, when and why we might never know. What did April say? We may be looking for a Socialised and Integrated Psychopath. We need to be in that flat. Have you called Cyril?"

"Is Sam the killer, is he the acid attacker, the murderer of Fella and Rhodes. Is he our Gideon?"

"Have you called Cyril?"

Chapter Thirty-Six

Phillips stood across from the vicarage. The house was in darkness apart from the side security lamp. The village streetlights were few and widely spread offering little light but that suited her. For now, the darkness was her friend. She slipped off the bag containing the hammer and nails and lodged it securely behind the fence. It would be inappropriate to take it to the pyramid. She approached the church, a walk she had taken many times. On this occasion, she experienced the usual feelings of anticipation and excitement but also some fear and sadness. This would be the last lesson, the final instruction and correction.

The small gate was closed as she stared at the clock 11.10. She would wait and watch, make sure there was no one about. There were few people during the day for goodness sake so it was highly unlikely that there would be anyone here at this time of night.

11.20 and she crossed the road and entered the churchyard. She followed the path and then turned round the back of the church, her eyes slowly growing accustomed to the limited light. When she saw the pyramid grave she stopped, her excitement increasing. Dropping the bag, she undressed before donning the brown, woollen robe. She removed the hat from her shaved head and what light there was shone on the taut flesh.

She knelt and then stood spreading her arms wide, her feet together; a human cross. The voice seemed weak but it was there drifting in the silence of the dark.

"You have done well, daughter, you have followed my commands and the corrections have been made. Some have learned and their lives will be richer, kinder. As we work to correct the weaknesses in others we gain strength ourselves.

You now only have the harlot, the whore to look to. Has she shown signs of change?"

Tracy called out. "She has but they occasionally still meet. I have seen and I have heard their fornications and their adulterous ways. I have witnessed their sexual immorality. She is in need of correction."

Her voice broke the silence of the churchyard.

John Barlow stood by the tree, his deliberate dark clothing masking his presence. It was to be his last patrol of the church and grounds for the evening and all had appeared quiet until he saw the hooded figure move to stand across the road from the church. He waited too to see what transpired. He then saw him cross the road and enter the churchyard. *Now what are you up to you son of a bitch? No good I can tell that!* He felt a flutter of excitement hit the pit of his stomach. He was even more surprised when the stranger removed something and started to strip before placing the discarded clothing in the bag. He had originally assumed it to be a male but even in the dim light he realised his mistake. Remaining motionless, conscious of how sound travels in the still of the night, he stood, fascinated. He had heard all about this Gideon character and if the opportunity came his way, he would have strong words. Here he was or should he say she? There was now silence; the silhouetted figure was still spread in the shape of the cross before the pyramid. He heard her speak again.

"Your will be done. I have heard and I will heed your command of correction and then I shall come to you. I am now growing fatigued and I am eager to be at your side."

***

Cyril arrived at the station. He had requested a car be sent as a precaution as he had been drinking. He had dropped Julie off before coming to the station. Rolling his electronic cigarette along his lips before inhaling helped calm him. He was angry at having to leave Julie, particularly after the support she had given him. Forwarded instructions for the team to be readied to search the flat were sent as he was approaching the station. He had requested two firearms specialists along with three officers, a sniffer dog and a small Forensic team. From all accounts the flat would be empty until the following day.

"We have an unmarked car at the site and all's quiet."

Cyril checked the clock behind the Reception desk. "We go at midnight. Have we had anything back from the sweep of Angie Rhodes's room?"

"I'll put someone on it and get back to you as soon as."

Cyril nodded.

***

Tracy Phillips brought her hands together and bowed. Barlow moved quickly from behind the tree. Maybe because she remained in a trance-like state or was just totally surprised, she simply stood as he approached. His arm shot out hitting her directly in the chest, pushing her backwards with some force until she stumbled and fell onto the grass. A short gasp exploded from her lips. He grabbed her before flicking her over bringing an arm up her back until he heard her moan in pain. He locked it by grabbing the rough, woollen material. It was a trick he had been taught in the Forces that allowed him to be in control. Slowly he brought her to her feet.

"Now who the fuck are you as you sure ain't Gideon Fletcher? Gideon from all accounts didn't have tits."

There was no response for a moment. "If anyone would come after me, he must deny himself and take up his cross daily and follow me," the chilled voice intoned.

Even though she was tall, he was a good three inches taller and much stronger. He lifted her a little using the locked arm and the same short gasps erupted from her lips as she struggled to her feet.

"You now have the choice between a dislocated shoulder or elbow or neither. Each is as easy for me to execute but none is pleasant other than the last option. Now let's try again. Who are you and what's going on in my churchyard?" To emphasise the point, he applied a little more pressure to her shoulder joint. She tried to rise on her toes to compensate.

"I'm here to receive instructions, just as Gideon received instructions, only he failed to follow them to the letter. He showed weakness. This will be the last time I come here. My work shall soon be done."

"And if you're not Gideon then who the hell are you?"

"I'm the one who brought correction to Gideon. My name is Hill, Sam Hill."

Barlow leaned and grabbed the bag. "You're coming with me. There are one or two things we need to discuss. Firstly I want information about a friend of mine. You may know him."

He marched her in front of the church and through the gate, her bare feet barely touching the ground.

Within minutes the light in the porch of his cottage illuminated them. He pushed her through the door before tossing the bag onto a chair.

"We need somewhere private for this little chat. As you've just experienced, you never know who's watching and listening in the darkest of places. If the one who talks to you is so powerful, I wonder why he didn't warn you I was there!"

***

The Force Control Room of the North Yorkshire Police was located at Fulford Road, York. They were aware of and co-ordinating the search and would be quick to reassure the public of the activities within the neighbourhood should calls to 101 or 999 calls come in. Getting this right was critical for securing the forensic evidence and keeping everyone safe. Cyril had performed such procedures many times but each brought its own anxiety. David Owen moved towards him with his thumb in the air.

"They've the big red key and ready on your say."

An officer was holding the ram that would be used to burst the locks on the door.

Cyril checked his watch. "One minute, everyone and no cock up. We must follow the procedure as discussed. Firearms Officers in first, then the dog, no one else enters unless they're clean. If in doubt keep safe."

Each station called its readiness and the door was shattered and the rooms cleared. As suspected, the flat was empty. However, the police dog was busy. A number of lights came on in the block and officers were quick to reassure the residents.

Cyril and Owen slipped on suits, gloves and overshoes. They were, in Cyril's eyes, now safe. Nothing in the flat appeared out of the ordinary other than the drugs that seemed secured in one room. The lounge was neat and orderly. Owen looked at two framed photographs on the fireplace. He pointed to one. "That is, if my memory serves me right, Tracy Phillips."

Cyril looked and agreed. He could not, however, make out who the other person was with her. Owen took out his phone and photographed it. The sudden flash made Cyril turn. "I'll be able to enlarge that and enhance it later. It might go through the facial recognition system too."

Cyril nodded, a cynical expression sweeping across his face. "Don't hold your breath, Owen."

"You might want to look in here, sir!" a voice from another room called.

Cyril responded immediately. An officer held open a wardrobe door and pointed to the hanging clothing.

"Thought Hill lived alone. There's a collection of men and women's clothing here. Look at the shoes!"

Cyril shone his torch into the lower area. The shoes were neatly paired and stacked. He carefully inspected them looking specifically at the size of a pair of women's shoes and comparing it with the man's. They were the same size.

"I want a full call out, get someone to the hospital, I need a detailed description of Hill from Baker. Circulate the photographs of Tracy Phillips to all traffic and foot patrols. Add to social media and I want a link to local news set for tomorrow morning. We need as much help from the public as we can muster. Send them over to the Merseyside Force. I want the prayer meeting checked. Shakti and Owen we need to have a word with Mrs Rhodes, she may be able to give a better description. I want everybody listed in this building to be questioned now. If they protest then they can be taken to the station."

Chapter Thirty-Seven

Tracy Phillips sat opposite Barlow, a look of total defiance clearly written across her face. The lights in the cottage gave a yellow glow to the room.

"I've seen you before. You were talking to Ian Fella by the pyramid grave. Seemed to me as though you weren't too happy. What was that all about?"

Tracy held the arm that had been forced up her back across her chest and cradled it with the other but said nothing.

"Did that little contretemps have anything to do with his death? A death that was clearly made to look like suicide but according to the police, the poor man was murdered. Was that your doing?"

***

Owen's phone rang. "Sir, acid attack on a youth on Ripon Market Square this evening, Nitric, as used on Kumar. There were two lads, one's fine and has given a reasonable description of the attacker. Someone claiming to be correcting them did it. Time of the blowing of the horn so about nine."

"Is it Gideon, Phillips or Hill? Maybe we're just looking for one person. Get a statement from the Hornblower and check with local hotels if anyone witnessed the incident." Owen lifted his phone. "Get them to see if anyone's reviewed their visit to the Hornblower on Trip Advisor. If so get them to follow it up."

"If it's Gideon, sir, they could be heading for Clipton. I'll get someone to check the pyramid grave and the church."

***

"The police showed me a photograph when I was at the station, asked if I'd seen a woman who'd been missing. Eighteen months, I think they said. You'll not believe this but that woman had a striking resemblance to the man I saw, let's say, arguing with Ian. Could have been her brother, I guess, but looking at you I'd have to be fucking stupid to believe that." He smiled, went to the sideboard and poured himself a scotch. She leaned across and grabbed her bag rummaging through it for the Jif lemon but without success. She stuffed the bag behind her. "I'd offer you one but I doubt those who do so much *correcting,* I think you said, would dream of taking alcohol." He turned and raised his glass.

Tracy looked directly at Barlow and smirked. "What are you going to do, call the police? No, you're too curious. You know I had a hand in your vicar's demise but I didn't put the noose around his neck, he did. Remember, if you give someone enough rope, they'll hang themselves. Fella was easy. He was a gentleman in every sense of the word. I met him a few times. He was troubled though. It was easy to make him believe that he was a failure. He'd shown weakness when Gideon used to visit him. They talked about his job and how he seemed to be a failure, to be stealing a living."

"Are you Gideon?"

She laughed. "Me?" She shook her head. "When I was working I would see the wrongdoings, people coming to the hotel illicitly, cheating under the guise of attending conferences with colleagues. You'd never believe what went on. The fornicators and the adulterers all collected under one roof. We had to clean up afterwards. Sexual immorality is rife. I was walking home after my shift and I met Gideon for the first time to speak to. I'd seen him on many occasions as he walked through the town. He handed me a page from the Bible. I read it and he stopped and talked. It was getting late and cold, and I asked if I could give him a meal and he accepted. I took him to my flat. Funny really, here I was, a single woman, taking a total stranger, some would say a strange stranger, back to my flat. It

205

never occurred to me that he'd do me any harm and he didn't. He stayed the night on the settee."

"What was on the page he gave you?"

"I know it by heart. *If anyone would come after me, he must deny himself and take up his cross daily and follow me.* It's from Luke. He'd stop with me often, and each time we'd talk. On one of his visits he told me of the pilgrimages he made to the pyramid grave and how he received orders of correction. I went with him and I heard them too. They were whispers at first but slowly they became discernible. It was from the voice of correction. I realised that Gideon was not what he professed to be, he was an eidolon."

John Barlow suddenly began to feel uncomfortable. The tight constraints of the cottage seemed to grow claustrophobic. "Eidolon... never heard of one."

She laughed. "He was totally false, his Christian ways were but a façade to carry on his evil ways. It was a deceit. He would gain trust and then abuse it."

"He didn't abuse you and from what you say he had the opportunity."

"He tried... once."

Barlow felt a chill run down his neck and his arms tingled. He'd met some evil people but she... In the light of the cottage, he felt as though he were staring into the eyes of evil.

"You've not asked about your friend, Reverend Ian Fella."

***

"That's all I can tell you. He kept himself to himself unless of course he was banging on the wall to get Angie to turn down her din!"

Cyril left, offering his apologies for the upset his visit might have caused. Shakti remained for a few more minutes.

"None of the other residents can shed any more light. Can't believe these people live so close to each other and nobody can tell us anything, Christ, he's out in the garden most days." Owen kicked a can that was on the driveway against the gable of the house. It disappeared down the narrow steps and lodged against the cellar door.

"Sir!" Shakti called in the darkness. Cyril and Owen returned to the door of Rhodes's flat. "She's just remembered, Angie sent her a selfie with Hill some time ago. She's checked the pictures on her phone but it's not there so she's checking back over her e-mails."

Owen looked at Cyril who immediately glanced towards the sky and whispered the words, "Please God."

"No, it's gone, sorry."

Cyril took a deep breath. "Get onto the phone people and see what they can drag up."

"We've already received them and the lab's going through them for any links to Gideon."

"Redirect the focus of the search. Fine tooth comb, Shakti."

As Cyril and Owen passed the front of the building, the light from the downstairs rooms flooded the garden, silhouetting the white forensics figures who were removing items and placing them into the back of a van.

"We'll not find anything in there other than the few prescription drugs the dogs found. My gut feeling says she's not coming back."

The officer standing by the driveway entrance moved to one side.

"Organise a rapid response CCTV trailer to monitor the front of the house. Full facial recognition and day-night surveillance, the full works. If she comes back I want an immediate alert. Pictures of everyone in the block to be added to the database for immediate crosscheck and ID."

"What about the rear of the property, anything there?"

"Anything to the side of the building will be picked up as they operate on a three hundred and sixty reference with automatic tracking and zoom. A fiver says she'll not return either as a male or female."

Owen smiled. "I'll take that."

***

Barlow leaned forward and stared at her. "So why kill him?"

"The day you saw us in the churchyard wasn't the first time we'd met. We'd talked about Gideon and Ian had shown me the envelope containing the passage wrapped with scarlet thread. That made me think about the thirteen human weaknesses but you already know his and he did too, the theft that he spoke of. That wasn't all, he held a secret sin even closer. I was informed at the pyramid and when I spoke of it to Fella his face was as red as the scarlet cord."

"And what sin was this?"

"He was a fornicator, a man of trust who fucked a married woman whilst her husband was away, not once but many times. It was this exposure, this hidden truth that made him realise that he was not only a thief but in the eyes of God he was a sinner. I knew what he would do, after all, he was a soldier and a brave one at that. I told him that I could shield those he cared about, his parishioners, from the sad truth. I would not tell. I watched him set it all up. He dressed beautifully, tidied the house before he moved into the garage. Each step was measured. He didn't speak, he just kept looking at me. I think he wanted me to tell him to stop, that everything would be all right. How could I do that when I'd been instructed to correct his ways?"

"We then moved to the garden. The evening was mild. There was a freshness to the air. We both sensed it. The evening light still lingered red and orange, enough to watch the events unfold. It was like a welcome, that he was being forgiven. I saw him stare at the beauty in the sky before he stood on the steps. Some cattle moved in the field behind the garden and gave us both a scare. He laughed! A man about to slip a rope around his own neck laughed. Everything was there, the rope and the steps even the hook on the back of the summerhouse that normally took the washing line. Do you know, I think there was a moment when he changed his mind but then I was quick enough to help, I was able to sweep the steps from beneath his feet. They tumbled away, clattering across the grass. Of course he tried to take the strain from the noose that bit into the tender flesh on his neck but that was impossible; your weight prevents that. Even with his feet against the wood of the summerhouse it proved to be unsuccessful."

She paused reflecting on the moment. "Have you ever seen someone slowly strangle? Someone fight to stay alive? It's not pretty. I put the note in his hand and tightened his grip after the thrashing had eventually stopped. You see, I wanted it found, just as I wanted the crosses to be discovered. Without those there'd be no point, no one would know why. There has to be a point to death as well as life don't you think? For these people to simply die would not teach others anything of what the Bible tells us."

"And the body found in the compost. Was that you too?"

"She helped. Dug her own grave. That's not strictly true, she shifted the compost and as a reward she then enjoyed a strong huff. Passed out and then I stripped her and I buried her. She wouldn't be able to shift the mesh, compost cage once I'd replaced it. It was easy."

"You're not on the side of good, you're one of the most evil, manipulative conniving people I've ever met..." He paused and blue-flashing lights lit the back wall briefly. He turned and went to the window. "Those are just the people I need to see. They're looking for you."

She shook her head. "I don't think so. I can hide behind Gideon. They're looking for a man. I'm just a missing statistic and certainly not a priority. Do you know how many missing people there are in the UK today?"

As she spoke she slipped her hand behind her and rummaged through the bag until she found the plastic lemon.

She withdrew it, flipped the lid and stood. Barlow moved his head trying to see if it was the police. She moved barefooted and silently to within a metre of Barlow.

"Is it the police?" Her voice was low and menacing. "How exciting!"

Barlow turned realising that she was behind him. The yellow object in her outstretched hand did not register immediately but as the stream of clear liquid struck its target, he gasped. He swung his hands trying to stop the flow or to connect with the hand but without success. She had the element of surprise on her side. He groaned as the acid etched further into the sensitive flesh in and around his eyes. The agony slowly intensified. He went down on one knee.

"I really didn't want to do that but I can't let you prevent me from fulfilling my final task." She moved through to the kitchen and immediately saw the knife block. "For your sake let's hope you keep them sharp," she said out loud.

Moving back into the small lounge she saw that Barlow was trying to stand, his hand on one chair as his other tried to hold his burning face. She picked up a small ornament and tossed it into the far corner of the room. It crashed against the wall. Barlow turned in the direction of the noise and in doing so exposed his back to her. She knew just where to place the knife and thrust the blade hard into the area of his right kidney. It slid silently catching bone on its journey, but travelling far enough to reach the handle before she twisted the blade with as much force as she could muster. An initial squeal was forced from his lips as a hand instinctively moved to the new area of agonising pain. Within seconds, he had folded and fallen to the floor, his head catching the corner of the chair as he did so. She moved towards the light switch, flicked it off and the room was plunged in darkness. The lights from the police car still patterned the wall but with a greater intensity. She would wait. Time and the night were on her side.

***

The officer moved the tape allowing the van and trailer to pull into the drive of the apartment block. The trailer camera was wheeled onto the grass and the operator secured the base before winding the handle to extend the cameras on a telescopic mast. It was soon operational. All movements would be automatically monitored and the control would be notified of any unusual activity. The facial recognition would also be constantly on the alert.

Chapter Thirty-Eight

The mobile phone danced across the auction house catalogue and then dropped onto the table as if chased by the shrill, ringing bell of an antique phone. Cyril lay back in the chair, his feet on another. The ringing seemed to be part of his dream. He had been home for an hour and considering the time, had not seen the point of retiring for the night. He had at least removed his trousers which were folded over a radiator and he had wrapped himself in a dressing gown. It had not taken him long to fall asleep but the nagging ring made him suddenly realise that it came from his own phone. He woke suddenly, quickly sitting up to see his glowing phone shimmy towards the edge of the table. He instinctively reached out a hand and caught it as it tumbled off the edge.

"Owz that?" he called raising his hands. Where this sudden burst of energy had come from he would never know.

He quickly answered. "Bennett." He listened carefully. "Shoes, male in the Clipton churchyard. How close to the pyramid? Has the camera been installed at..." He didn't have time to finish. "...that's something at least."

Cyril stood, collected his trousers and put them over his arm. "Has anyone called in on John Barlow, the church caretaker, to see if he's seen anything? No? Just get someone there. His address is on file. Send me a car in fifteen minutes and I want DC Richmond and DS Owen in it when it arrives here. Yes, I am aware of the time, sergeant." He put his head in his free hand and rubbed his face, suddenly realising that he was creasing his trousers. He placed the phone on the sideboard. "It's simple policing for goodness sake!" he grumbled as he went into the kitchen. He slipped a pod into the coffee machine before going into the bathroom to shower and shave.

Checking his watch, he pressed the button to start the coffee machine and he watched the stream of dark, black coffee pour into the espresso cup, the aroma immediately lifting his spirits. His phone rang as he raised the cup and sipped.

"Bennett." The voice sounded anxious. "Bloody hell!" He listened as the details of Barlow's plight were relayed to him. "Have we an estimated time of death? Between midnight and two?" He checked his watch again. 5.57. "So this could've been taking place whilst the police were actually in the churchyard?" He shook his head.

The doorbell rang. Cyril hung up, finished his coffee and grabbed his coat and jacket before going to the door, tapping his pockets to make sure he had everything he needed. He mumbled inaudibly his mental checklist to ensure that he had forgotten nothing; *spectacles, testicles wallet and watch* before opening the door to be greeted by Owen. Cyril climbed into the front and nodded to the driver. April was in the rear.

"I take it you've heard, sir. Barlow. Acid and then knifed. Forensics is on the way as is Dr Pritchett. The youth who witnessed the attack on Ripon Market Square has given us a pretty bland description as usual a hooded figure but I think to save face he's exaggerated the attacker's size and build. Six five, heavy set, tattoos." Owen raised his eyebrows. "Could've been me if it weren't for the tattoos." He laughed at his own joke and April smiled politely. Cyril watched the road. "We also found someone who'd posted a review on Trip Advisor saying that the two youths were disrupting the horn-blowing ceremony, revving their bikes as loudly as possible. The person in question had gone to stop them. They described a true knight in shining armour who bravely tackled the two yobs. Gave the Hornblower five stars!"

"Description, Owen? I don't care if he gave it a bloody constellation. Did he give us a description of Sir Lancelot?"

"Total contradiction to that given by the yob. Woollen hat pulled well down, about six foot and carrying two bags. One

213

looked particularly heavy. Went off down Kirkgate after sorting out the trouble."

There was a pause as the driver negotiated the two roundabouts at Ripley. Cyril slid open one of the windows. To turn and look at either in the back would only induce carsickness.

He inhaled some fresh air. "You're up to speed I take it? Looks like Hill is Phillips and Phillips may well be Gideon, or at least taking on the guise of Gideon."

"Yes."

***

Realising she had left her shoes by the grave, she had rummaged around until she found a pair of Barlow's and some socks. With the addition of three pairs of thick socks they would do. She had remained dressed in Gideon's guise as it somehow seemed appropriate. She had left the cottage soon after the blue lights had disappeared, deciding to leave her shoes behind. If they were still there, it mattered not. She needed the hammer. She had been cautious in case they had left an officer on watch but then why should they? All had been quiet. She was right. The street was empty and the bag was where she had left it.

The walk to the next village had been easier than she had anticipated. A solitary car and a van had passed her but the lights had warned of their approach and she had managed to hide in the hedgerow. As she approached the village, she glanced at the sky and took a moment to marvel at the myriad stars that were so clear. The sheer scale always filled her with awe. She contemplated her journey, her reward for the work she had done here on earth. He had told her of the rich rewards that awaited her. She quickened her step. She spied the village shop. She was now close. Her hand felt the weight of the hammer through the thick wall of the bag. The house she was looking for was just across the road, Rahab, the harlot's home, was sited next to the church wall.

214

The dawn light was just beginning to break but the street remained dark and quiet. The low light from the fridges and from the blue insect killer in the shop glowed out of the large windows lighting the pavement blue.

She would wait in the church where it would be safe; after all, she had the key taken from Ian Fella's house on the night he died. She wondered how the police could possibly have missed that but then they had missed opportunities on several occasions.

Crossing the street she entered the churchyard. The large, oak doors were hidden within a shallow porch. She took the key from her bag and inserted it as quietly as possible. As she turned the handle and pushed, the hinges protested as she felt the cool air rush past her in escape. The darkness enfolded her as the door closed and locking it, she suddenly felt secure for the first time that evening. At seven *she* would come, she would prepare the church for the eight o'clock service for the stand-in vicar.

***

Cyril saw the blue strobe lights as they approached Clipton. He spotted Julie's car and the white-coated ghostly figures changed from white to blue as they were struck by the cars' strobe lights. Owen was the first to get out but April remained seated. Cyril opened his door, relieved the journey was over but then realised that April had not moved.

"Are you all right? You must find Clipton a little like Midsomer, what with the two deaths." He tried to lighten the mood turning to look at her. Her face, illuminated by the roof courtesy light, showed that she was deep in thought.

"I have a feeling that we shouldn't be here, we're too late. I think we should be with Mrs Fleet. I don't know why but... I keep getting these goose bumps whenever I think about her. The village shopkeeper said that she was a bit of a one for the men and maybe the vicar was... I don't know. Maybe it's just me."

Cyril got out of the car and called after Owen who turned quickly. Cyril, waved his hand, beckoning his return as he glanced at the church clock. It was 6.50.

"Owen, get in! April, when in doubt do the courageous thing. What would you have me do?"

"Mrs Fleet, sir."

Owen did not demur. He could see from April's expression that she was troubled. The car sped down Clipton's main street.

***

The key hitting the escutcheon plate seemed to be amplified within the emptiness of the church making Tracy Phillips jump and then stand. She adjusted the rope that was tied around her waist and picked up the plastic lemon that she had positioned on the end pew. The door slowly opened and she saw Mrs Fleet come in.

She held a small torch. Closing the door, she moved across to the light switch. As the single row of lights came on she turned off the torch and returned to lock the door. After Reverend Fella's death she could never be too careful. Satisfied that she was secure, she turned. A slight scream of surprise burst from her lips as she saw the bowed and hooded figure standing in front of her. In the distance a deep bark emerged. Ralph had heard the scream.

Tracy looked up and stared but she did not give Mrs Fleet time to speak or scream again. She squeezed the lemon sending a stream of acid directly into her face. Mrs Fleet dropped her torch as her hands went immediately to her eyes. As the acid burned, the scream already on her lips intensified. The dog's deep bark could again be heard.

Tracy pulled the hammer and the horseshoe nails from her bag, slipped three of the nails between her lips like shiny

216

metal fangs, before moving towards the stricken, blind Mrs Fleet. Grabbing her left wrist she forced it against the wooden door. Slumped on the floor as she was, her arms were weightless. Taking one of the nails she forced the point onto the skin and pushed. The nail penetrated Mrs Fleet's flesh between the two bones with ease until it touched the timber. The force of the hammer blow on the nail's flat head finished the job, pinning her arm to the wood. Tracy quickly grabbed her other arm, spread it out and repeated the procedure. Two small streams of blood began to flow from the punctured skin, running down along her arms until reaching her elbows where they pooled and dripped onto the tiles. Tracy stood back and looked at the crucified woman who writhed in agony. No scream erupted from her lips, only gasps as she tried to draw in air. Her head hung low to her right owing to her body's position, her feet folded beneath her.

Tracy brought the small, wooden cross from her bag.

"A harlot's cross. A spy in God's house, a sinner, but He saw and He knew. You shall be crossed out, corrected just like Kumar, like Fella and like Rhodes. You have all allowed your weaknesses to control your judgements."

The lights from the car coming down the street flashed vivid colours on the church wall from the row of stained glass windows. The noise of the opening doors accompanied by voices broke the silence. The deep bark from Mrs Fleet's dog could be heard again, this time, more frantic.

"The church, the lights! She's in the church!" April screamed as she jumped the wall and ran to the door. "It's locked, sir." She banged on the door and heard the sound amplified within.

Owen grabbed Cyril. "My shoulders, you should be able to see into the church."

Cyril climbed onto the wall. He then placed one foot on each of Owen's shoulders whilst holding Owen's hands. They moved carefully until Cyril held the stone mullion on either side of the window. He placed his face close to the glass and rubbed it with his sleeve. He could see in. It took him a few moments to comprehend fully and absorb the scene.

"Bloody hell!" Cyril exclaimed as he stared at Mrs Fleet's slumped torso. "Hill's crucified Fleet to the door!"

Owen looked up as he held his hands against the wall to steady himself.

"April back up and medic, now and find a way into this place. Quickly!"

She called it in and then approached the nearby shop. She had noticed that the curtains were partly open and a face, illuminated by the streetlight, looked out at the commotion below. April banged on the door. Within seconds, the upstairs light came on followed by those of the shop. April recognised the woman who stood brandishing what looked like a poker. Holding her ID flat against the glass of the door, April she shouted, "Police!"

***

Cyril managed to take his eyes away from Mrs Fleet and then he saw the Gideon figure. He watched through the dirt-streaked glass as the figure walked up to Mrs Fleet's now motionless body. She placed the cross against her left temple, the nail having already been tapped in place and lifted the hammer.

"No!" Cyril screamed banging on the glass as the nail penetrated the wood and the side of the woman's skull.

Tracy swung the hammer again ensuring that the nail gained maximum penetration before turning to look directly at the distorted face that stared in.

"What's going on, sir?" Owen shouted, feeling Cyril's weight as he banged the window.

At that moment, the hammer crashed through the glass close to Cyril's face forcing the window to shatter and break free from the lead that held it in place. Cyril wobbled but managed to grab hold of the stone mullion. As he turned his head, the aperture gave a perfectly clear view. Tracy Phillips stood looking directly at him, her arms above her head. In her hands she held a kitchen knife.

***

The shopkeeper opened the door. "Police! Does anyone have a key for the church other than Mrs Fleet? It's an emergency."

The woman turned, went through the back and returned with a key. "It's not the front door it's the side, there on the right."

April grabbed the key and dashed back across the road.

***

Phillips brought the knife round slowly and positioned it on her chest. As if in slow motion, she fell forwards, the blade plunging deep within her chest. Cyril watched as her body twitched and the legs kicked spasmodically. Slowly a dark patch oozed from beneath the now still body. It was then that he noticed April.

"Check Mrs Fleet for a pulse!"

She looked up and shook her head.

Cyril leaned against the wall. "I need to come down, there's nothing more we can do."

Chapter Thirty-Nine

Cyril watched from the car as the CSI moved into the church. As he had been witness to what had transpired, their work would not take long. He closed his eyes and tried to ignore the sound of the police radio as he replayed the events that he had just witnessed. There was something missing. If Hill, AKA Phillips had not been in Southport then where had he been?

At that moment Owen opened the door. "Owner of Hill's flat called in. There's a cellar there, you need to take a look!" Owen handed Cyril an iPad. The centre of the screen showed a white circle and a triangle. Sliding his finger on the screen, he tapped. Cyril watched as the camera panned around the room. It paused on the large, wooden cross before focussing on each of the nailed photographs. Studying each one, Cyril paused the screen. Owen watched over his shoulder, having already seen it.

"That's Tracy Phillips with Gideon Fletcher. It was taken on The Stray. If you look behind them you should be able to make out the banner detailing The Tour so from that we can date this picture. It's about the time they both went missing. The nail holding that photograph is a horse shoe nail just like those used on Mrs Fleet."

"I wonder where the bastard is now?"

"Just keep watching, all will be revealed. The next photo's interesting too."

Cyril tapped *play* and the video resumed. When the next image came into shot, he paused it.

"Tracy Phillips, Gideon and Fella by the pyramid grave. What the...?"

"Look at the trees! That was taken in autumn. We'll check to see if they've been photoshopped when they're back at the lab, you just don't know these days."

Cyril continued with the video.

"Kumar's car and…?" Owen pointed out.

"That's Angie Rhodes, isn't it?"

"Yep! If you look, the rear window is smashed on the car so it was taken after Kumar was doused in acid. She was the bait. There's more."

There were photographs of Ian Fella standing in Mrs Fleet's garden surrounded by bantams, Ralph standing next to him as they embraced. Next was a close-up photograph of Fella's face. The distorted features had clearly been captured after his hanging. The last photograph proved the most puzzling. It was a close up of Gideon's face. His eyes were closed but it was clear from the infestation around the nostrils and mouth and the flesh tint that they were looking at a decomposing corpse.

"Gideon Fletcher! Is he in the cellar?" Cyril asked inspecting the photograph more closely.

"Not found as yet. There's acid, and hair samples that match the scarlet dye from the crosses. They're doing a DNA sweep and hopefully that'll confirm that both Phillips and Fletcher have been there."

Chapter Forty

Julie drove down Wybunbury Lane. They had stopped in Nantwich for Cyril to have a beer and consider his next step. He had walked around the centre and looked at the church before making the decision to continue.

"It's coming up on the right," he said. The trees and the lane seemed so familiar to him even after the many years. "Things so far out in the countryside never seem to change."

Julie saw the gate and set back from it the red brick house. She stopped to let a car pull out of the drive before turning in. The gravel crunched reassuringly under the wheels as she swung the car round on the grass circle bringing it to a halt opposite the door. She studied the beautiful house, it reminded her of Cyril; it was immaculate. The creeper was trimmed to the same level and the cream painted wood complemented the coloured brick. Nothing was out of place.

Cyril sat looking forward. He could see his past running before him in his mind's eye, the bicycle, the pony, his father's Bentley.

The front door opened and Julie saw an elderly lady standing on the top step. She smiled. Julie climbed from the car and went to meet her.

"I didn't think he would come," she said as she shook Julie's hand gently. "I'm Wendy. I'm so glad he's here."

Cyril walked up the steps. There was no smile, no warmth only good manners as he shook Wendy's outstretched hand.

"He's in the lounge, Cyril. He may be sleeping. The nurse has just left. She checks him and gives him medication for the pain."

Julie put her hand on his shoulder as he went into the hallway before disappearing through the large double doors to the right.

"Come into the kitchen, you'll be ready for some tea."

They sat at the oak table, each with a cup and saucer as Wendy poured tea from the Picquot ware teapot. There was a moment's silence and then Wendy spoke.

"His mother planned all of this." She laughed to herself. "She and I were such close friends and we were both in love with the same man. Sadly, he didn't choose me but we all remained good friends. Yes, I met a number of eligible young men but... Anyway, when Cyril's mother became ill I came to help; she was, after all, my best friend. It was then that we talked and she told me that she was dying and was fearful for Cyril. She asked me to have an affair with Cyril's father. Obviously I protested but inside I must admit I was so excited. One thing led to another. I eventually moved in to care for her."

"At first Cyril was fine but suddenly he changed, he wouldn't speak to me, he became withdrawn. It was the weekend that he was going to see an air show. He was so excited. After that he changed. I found out much later why. His mother wanted someone there for him when she'd gone, to treat him as only a mother could. Julie, I tried so very hard to make him love me but..."

Cyril entered the kitchen. He was holding some papers and a photograph. He dropped them on the table and Julie could see it was a photograph of his mother. He turned it over and pushed it towards Julie. The writing was spidery and uncertain. She read it.

My darling Cyril,
If you are reading this I know that you are now a grown man. I hope these tender words will find a place in your heart and that you will show compassion. I know your love of aircraft and the brave pilots and Jan Smuts' words inspired one such pilot, Peter Isaacson. These words have stayed in my heart and

helped me to make the most difficult of decisions. I write it for you so that you might understand.

'When in doubt, do the courageous thing.'

I knew that I would not be here to love the two most important people in my life. God had denied me that but what he was going to take with one hand he offered to give back a lifeline with the other; he gave me Wendy, a loving friend and confidante. It was just like those circumstances that befell our favourite composer! I was aware that she adored your father and that she loved you. I knew that she would guide and help you. Suddenly I had a hope and I had the power to ensure that both you and your father would be loved, not for financial gain, but by a woman I loved, a woman I knew felt a real love for him. Cyril, I hope that you will realise that it was done with the best of intentions. It was the most difficult decision I ever have had to make but it is one that could only have been made with a mother's love. If you ever read this I hope that you will understand.

Your most loving mother

xx

PS I'm sure that your father and Wendy are as proud of you as I am. I can hear the lark ascending and I must follow. Until we meet again, my darling boy. Like the pilots you so admired, be brave, be honest but above all be true to yourself.

X

Julie could feel the emotion well in her stomach. She was afraid to look at Cyril in case she burst into tears. He moved around the table and held Wendy by her shoulders before leaning and placing a kiss on her forehead. He smiled at her.

He walked across the courtyard and opened the side door to the expansive garage. It was there, the Bentley, covered in two large dustsheets. He opened the garage doors to allow the light to flood in before carefully removing the covers. A cable ran to the battery from a trickle charger which he disconnected, then he opened the door. He smiled as it opened the opposite way to modern cars. He turned the key and the engine juddered slowly before bursting into life. Clouds of grey exhaust curled and slowly filled the garage. He moved the column shift and allowed the maroon behemoth to edge into the daylight. Parking it directly in front of the lounge window, he returned to his father. He helped to lift the frail, old man so that he could look out of the window. His discomfort was clear, but as he saw the car, pleasure suddenly flushed across his face. Cyril watched as he closed his eyes. He lowered his head gently back onto the pillow.

"Thank you, my son. Thank you for coming."

Chapter Forty-One

Cyril sat in his office as he read Wendy's letter informing him of his father's death. He did not feel any sadness. He had done the right thing. Suddenly the light disappeared from the room as Owen stood in the doorway.

"You're like an ambling alp, Owen! Come in and sit and bring the light with you." He held out his hand. "Fiver, and not from your back pocket. Phillips never returned to the flat and therefore neither did Hill. We had a wager, remember?"

Owen opened his wallet and handed it over. Cyril smiled.

"What's with the *ambling alp* by the way?"

"Primo Carnera, Italian World Heavyweight Champion. You get my drift, Owen?"

Owen appeared confused so returned to safer ground... the case.

"Cadaver dogs have searched the site but with no success. DNA shows that Gideon Fletcher had used the cellar and the front flat. It was also found in Angie Rhodes's room. Semen. Not as God fearing as he wanted everyone to believe. What did April call them?"

"Socialised and Integrated Psychopaths. It appears from the evidence we had two. Likes attract!" Cyril smiled.

"I felt sorry for Ian Fella, didn't deserve that and neither did Mrs Fleet. Did you know April's taken the dog, Ralph; he's like a small donkey. Christ knows where she'll keep him. Mrs Fleet's husband asked her if she wanted him as he's away so often. Didn't seem to take the news of her adultery badly. Said he knew and told Fella he did. I'd have knocked Fella's block off if it were me!"

Cyril smiled considering the irony. "There were too many coincidences, Owen, far too many. Some may well have been contrived." He picked up the letter and smiled. "Or if we return to the parlance of the Bible, one begat the other."

"What about Graham Baker?"

"Owen, you're not married for that number of years without developing a real strength. He's a statistic of an over-burdened National Health Service. He'll face charges but he'll receive only a suspended sentence, nothing more. He's a victim just like Ian Fella and Mrs Fleet. Crime always leaves victims in its wake. Our job is to separate fact from fiction." He smiled to himself. "Coach and Horses?" Cyril held up the fiver. "This prodigal son would like to make his acquaintance with a certain Black Sheep."

"If you're buying, I'm drinking." Owen rubbed his hands.

"I take it you've heard that April has applied to be with us permanently?"

"Even more reason to celebrate. She's good. Shall I get Shakti?"

Cyril smiled. "She can be the rose, Owen."

Featured Artist

John Thompson

(1924 – 2011)

'do you like 'em then?'

John was born in Oldham, Lancashire, an artist who only became popular late in life. However, when success came it came quickly and he was to become one of the best-selling living artists in the UK. His work hangs in the Houses of Parliament.

John is famous for his group images depicting northern folk, predominantly men. His group work was numbered rather than titled. Many of his sketches were given humorous, handwritten titles. The one mentioned in this book, 'It's not in my pocket', depicts a line of people frantically rummaging through their pockets.

John was a self-taught artist of great wit and charm. He has often been referred to as Oldham's Lowry.

A book was published about John entitled **"do you like 'em then?"** written by Stuart Archer and Bill Clark

Acknowledgements

The conclusion of 'Crossed Out' and I have so many people to thank for their support and guidance. Naïvely, I thought that the more you write the easier it would become. How wrong could I have been! For one, there is a responsibility to make sure that the characters develop and that they work well together. It has been great fun introducing April Richmond to the team in this book. I believe it is also important to reveal a little more of Cyril's past, a past that up to this point has been concealed. I hope that you are enjoying discovering a little more about Cyril. Julie certainly is!

For the time I'm writing a new Bennett book, my mind is in this fictitious world, much to the amusement of my wife, Debbie, who now knows where I drift when I should be listening! Her unfailing belief is the reason I'm here. Who would have believed we are already at book six?

Now for the many words of thanks.

To Debbie, Carrie, Barbara, Stef, Christopher and Kath for reading through the final draft and offering your corrections. There's that word again! Fortunately, the consequences are a little less severe! I offer you all a huge thank you.

To Gary, my thanks for your clear advice on the handling and effects of the acids mentioned.

To Jim Ashcroft for your technical advice. I'd have made some foolish mistakes without it.

To Ian Fella. Thank you. I hope you like your character.

I'm grateful to so many wonderful bloggers who help promote my writing. However, I must thank, as always, Caroline

Vincent, who has been my guiding light and a strong advocate of the Bennett books from the beginning, Susan Hampson, Kath Middleton, Susan Hunter, Emma Mitchell, Sarah Hardy, Sarah Kenny, Shell Baker, Sue Harrison, Monica Mac, Maxine Groves, Helen Claire, Beverley Ann Hopper, Noelle Holten. If I have missed anyone, please accept my apologies.

A thank you too to the many book groups who regularly mention the Bennett series in their posts.

Thanks must also go to Imagined Things Bookshop, Harrogate.

Finally, last but not least may I thank you, the reader. I know many of you have followed Bennett through every case with real enthusiasm. Forgive me but I must add a particular mention to Donna Wilbor, Livia Sbarbaro, Dee Williams, Geoff Blakesley and Kathryn Wilkinson. I'm so pleased you found my books.

Peter Stuart Isaacson, AM, DFC, AFC, DFM
(31 July 1920 – 7 April 2017)

Stationed at Breighton, Yorkshire with 460 Squadron RAAF

If you have a minute, please read up about this man's life. He was inspired by this quote:

"When in doubt, do the courageous thing."

Jan Smuts

www.malcolmhollingdrakeauthor.co.uk
www.malcolmhollingdrakeauthor.com

Crossed Out

Malcolm Hollingdrake

Printed in Great Britain
by Amazon